A STEAMY ALIEN MONSTER ROMANCE

CRUSHING CINZA

LEANN RYANS | V.T. BONDS
USA Today Bestselling Authors

Copyright © 2021 Leann Ryans and V.T. Bonds

Cover design by Getcovers.com.

All rights reserved.

No part of this book may be reproduced in any form or by any electronic or mechanical means, including information storage and retrieval systems, without written permission from the author, except for the use of brief quotations in a book review.

***

For more books by Leann Ryans in a variety of worlds, check out https://leannryans.com.

***

Go to https://vtbonds.com for a complete list of books by V.T. Bonds.

For new releases, discounts, and Knotty Exclusives, subscribe to V.T. Bonds' newsletter at

https://vtbonds.com/newslettersubscriber.

Contents

Chapter 1 9
Chapter 2 19
Chapter 3 27
Chapter 4 35
Chapter 5 45
Chapter 6 51
Chapter 7 59
Chapter 8 73
Chapter 9 87
Chapter 10 97
Chapter 11 107
Chapter 12 115
Chapter 13 121
Chapter 14 131
Chapter 15 145
Chapter 16 151
Chapter 17 159
Chapter 18 167
Chapter 19 181
Chapter 20 193
Chapter 21 203

Chapter 22	209
Epilogue	215
Author's Note	221
Enslaving Ezmira (Preview)	225
Unknown Omega by V.T. Bonds (Preview)	231
Monster's Find by Leann Ryans (Preview)	237
Rescued and Ruined by V.T. Bonds (Preview)	245
Tempting A Knight by Leann Ryans (Preview)	253
Follow V.T. Bonds	259
Follow Leann Ryans	263

Chapter 1

Cinza

Pain shot into Cinza's shoulders and infected her spine as she caught her fall with her forearms. The marble floor sapped the heat from her front, easing the agony in her bones, but the hall's regulated air conditioning wafted the scent of her own fear into her nostrils. Gritting her teeth in embarrassment as her squeak of alarm bounced off the high ceiling, Cinza sucked in a breath through her nose before turning her head to look up at her tormentor.

Golden irises beamed from a face full of mischief, Armyn's raised eyebrow mocking her even as his cheek twitched. An expression flashed across his features before he settled them into a decidedly uncaring facade. It wouldn't have fit on any of the other kids his age, but Armyn pulled it off with ease.

Royalty came with many privileges and perks, and since he was the king's son, the eight-year-old oozed more strength and self-assurance than most grown men.

Cinza pushed into a sitting position and cradled her elbow to her torso, the sharp pain worrying her even as her eyes darted around to make sure no one had seen. Her class had only graduated to this side of the building two weeks ago, most of her peers turning six long before she had. It sucked to be the youngest in her class, but her teacher said she was a fast learner.

"Why'd you push me?"

His eyes darkened at her words, the bright blue of his flesh highlighting the change as he leaned over her.

"Did you just accuse me of something?"

"I-I... but you—"

"I was just coming over to help you up after you tripped over nothing."

Prince Armyn stepped even closer, nudging her thigh with the side of his taloned foot as he extended his hand. Offering his palm, he stared into her eyes and waited for her to take it.

Remembering how he'd pulled her hair so hard she'd almost cried at the school's year-opening ceremony, Cinza hesitated. He'd pretended like he hadn't yanked her ponytail, but her scalp still ached from his tug.

But then he'd been really nice a few days ago when she'd been late to class and had dropped her satchel. Her books had scattered all over the hall, and as she'd dropped to her knees to get them, he'd shown up out of nowhere and helped her pick them up.

He had said nothing, but the way he'd searched her eyes before he'd walked away… Cinza still didn't know what he'd been trying to find.

When she took too long to lay her hand on his, his eyes hardened. Cinza's stomach dropped to her feet, but when he didn't move his hand away, she tentatively raised hers so he could help her.

Before their fingers made contact, a derisive snort sounded from behind Armyn.

"Oh look! Cinza fell. *Again*."

Quasim's green feathers came into view as he sauntered around his best friend and flicked his wing in a display of annoyance. The gesture couldn't have been more manly if the prince's bodyguard-to-be had been full grown. The males' mannerisms mimicked those in charge, since their entire lives revolved around the responsibilities they'd shoulder in the future—they'd already begun training their bodies for battle.

Cinza fought not to cower, but having both older boys looming over her was frightening.

"You're so *clumsy* and frail."

Armyn's neck swiveled until he stared at Quasim's profile, the hand so near to Cinza's closing into a fist, but the other boy didn't seem to notice.

"How is someone so *stupid* still ali—"

A flash of blue streaked across Cinza's vision before Armyn's fist landed in the very center of Quasim's face. Flying backward from the impact, Quasim's wings spread just in time for his butt to hit the floor. His hands hid his shock as he tried to stop the blood gushing from his nose, but crimson flowed down his chin and dripped onto his once-pristine white shirt.

Turning to face his laid-out friend, Armyn balled his hands into fists again and scowled.

"No! You don't get to be mean to her."

After looking between his prince and Cinza a few times, Quasim's eyebrows scrunched before smoothing into lines of acceptance. When he shifted to stand, Armyn stepped closer to him and snarled.

"You'll treat her with respect and protect her, no matter what. Understand?"

Quasim turned his gaze to Cinza, his eyes squinting in confusion again before he snapped his attention back to Armyn when the prince growled.

"I hear you, my prince. Understood."

"Good. Now get out of here before I punch you again."

Quasim stood and shook out his feathers as he stomped away, wisely keeping his mouth shut even though his nose left droplets of blood behind him.

Golden eyes swung back toward her before he shook the hand he'd clocked his best friend with.

"He's got a face as hard as iron."

Armyn offered his palm again as a smirk slid across his face. Cinza laid hers in his before she realized she'd moved. The zap of electricity running up her arm made her pounding heart ache, his touch so warm and full of strength she didn't know what to do with it. Her cheeks heated, no doubt causing a bright red flush on her pale skin, so she looked away and tried to pretend she didn't feel so weird.

"Remember that if you ever need to hit him, okay?"

Not understanding what he meant because she couldn't remember what he'd said before, Cinza scrunched her nose and glanced at him.

"What?"

"If he ever messes with you, don't aim for his face. Kick him in the balls."

Cinza's feet tried to shuffle away, the thought of hurting someone else making her feel queasy.

Fingers pinched her chin and forced her to look into shimmering golden eyes.

"But he won't mess with you ever again. I promise."

Without another word, he slid his fingers off her face as he stepped away, his hand releasing hers at the same time. He turned and took a step away from her before a group of kids from his grade turned into the hallway. The noise shocked Cinza into movement, her shoes squeaking on the floor as she tried to hurry back to class.

Despite taking a wide path around Armyn to go down the hall, his wing shot out at the last second and knocked her sideways.

With his powerful punch replaying in her mind, Cinza bounced off the wall and twisted to avoid banging into him. His forearm shot out and stopped her descent, but her feet popped out from under her, leaving all her weight on his arm for a few heart stopping seconds. As she tucked her feet back under herself and regained her balance, silence spread through the hallway.

"Watch where you're going, Tiny."

Feeling the older kids staring at her as adrenaline coursed through her veins, anger rose so fast and fierce her entire face felt like it would burst into flames. Not knowing what to make of his actions, Cinza glared up at her future king and scowled. His mood swings were giving her whiplash.

Unable to form any words, she jerked away from his arm and fled down the hall, tucking her wings straight behind her and hunching her shoulders, hoping to disappear.

Everyone always made fun of her because she was tiny. Maybe if she shrank a little more, she'd become invisible, and Prince Armyn would leave her alone.

Except, as she turned the corner to flee to her classroom, her eyes sought his striking wings and proud stance. His golden eyes captured hers until the wall broke their line of sight, the myriad of emotions swirling in them too fraught for her to dissect.

She liked him when he was kind to her, which only seemed to happen when they were alone, but didn't know what to do when he was mean. And she didn't understand why he had punched Quasim—she heard much worse from other kids in the school.

Her parents became high class through work, not blood, which painted a target on her thin wings whether she did something wrong or remained above reproach. Especially because she looked so different compared to most of them.

In a way, what Quasim said was true—she *was* frail. She'd had to visit the nurse last week when her wing had torn during their first physical education class of the year. She'd healed since then, but Cinza had wanted to crawl in a hole and die when she'd cried in front of the entire class because it hurt so much.

At least now she didn't have to play any sports. She could just walk the garden or fly laps around the track.

Knocking on her classroom door before opening it, Cinza turned in her hall pass before sitting in her seat, nodding when the teacher asked if everything was okay. After thanking Cinza for being so responsible, the woman returned to teaching the lesson.

Cinza always sat in the front row, otherwise she wouldn't be able to see around her classmates, and it helped lessen the distractions of the classroom. She couldn't see the way they pointed and whispered if they were behind her.

While middle- and lower-class students her age learned basic letters and numbers, society expected the members of royalty and the upper-class to be much more advanced, which suited Cinza more than she could say. Learning fed her soul, so it was easy to sink into the lesson, no matter what subject was being taught.

After flipping the pages of her book so she was in the right section, Cinza tried to push the events of the hallway from her mind but couldn't get

Armyn's golden eyes and mischievous smirk out of her thoughts.
    Why couldn't he just leave her alone?

Chapter 2

Armyn

"So the innocent little Fayrie gets naughty sometimes, and I caught her."

Armyn leaned his shoulders back against the doorframe and crossed his arms as he watched the young teen shove the giant sweet roll into her mouth. He'd startled her to see what she'd do, sneaking up close before making a sound.

He hadn't had the chance to pick on her in almost two years, the longest span of time since he'd started eight years prior, so finding her doing something wrong was too perfect an opportunity to pass up. Huge silvery-blue eyes turned to stare up at him, the hand over her lips not covering all the icing smeared on her cheeks and chin.

He couldn't help the smirk that crossed his face. She was adorable.

"I—"

Cinza tried to talk, whether to argue her innocence or plead forgiveness he didn't know, but she choked before she could get out more than a word. Darting to the sink, Armyn grabbed a glass and filled it with water, passing it to her in silence when she continued to cough. She drained it, finally forcing down the last of the gooey dough.

"I-I didn't mean... They just smelled so good."

Armyn stepped closer, pressing a finger to her lips to hush her. Sticky sweetness smeared on his digit, and when she stopped trying to talk, he brought it to his mouth, licking it off as he kept his eyes on Cinza.

Cheeks flushing a bright shade of pink, she looked away. He had to remind himself she was younger than him and stealing a kiss from those pouty lips would be inappropriate, even if he was only a teen himself.

"It's nice to see you're not as good as everyone thinks. Makes you more... mortal."

He reached out and gripped her chin. Forcing her to look up at him once again, he grabbed the towel from the table beside them and reached back to the sink to wet it. Raising it to her face, he gently wiped away the evidence of her theft.

"Are you going to tell on me?"

Crushing Cinza

She trembled in his grip, her arms wrapping around her ribs. As a diplomat's daughter, anything she did reflected on her father, and while Armyn knew Administrator Glashu was a fair man, he was also stern. He might ban her from coming to the palace with him, and Armyn didn't want that. Their age difference meant they shared no classes, and the extra time she spent in the halls was his only chance to get close to her.

The stomp of footsteps coming down the stairs at the opposite end of the room stole their attention. Cinza's breath caught, her trembling growing more intense. The theft of a roll might not seem like much, but Cook ruled the kitchen with an iron fist, and he wasn't shy about whacking people with his wooden spoon. The thought of seeing her flesh turn purple from the alpha's hit made Armyn want to punch the man, even though Cook had never had reason to strike Cinza before.

The burly male would also drag Cinza straight to her father, which meant Armyn might not see her for a long time. He already didn't get to see her as often as he'd like.

Sliding his hand to Cinza's shoulder, he reached down and lifted the cloth covering the table beside them.

He pushed her as he hissed out, "Hide."

"But..."

Those silvery-blue eyes locked on him, lips parted and tempting him once again. Shaking his head, Armyn gave another push down on her shoulder, forcing her to drop to her knees. He released the tablecloth as she shuffled underneath, reaching for a sweet roll with the other hand and cramming a huge bite into his mouth.

It really was delicious. He wondered if Cinza's lips would taste as good.

Being sure to smear icing on his cheeks and drop crumbs on his vest so it looked like he'd had more, Armyn pretended to turn to run as Cook came into view.

"Stop right there."

Cook's voice boomed through the small kitchen. He used the larger one across the hall when they were entertaining and he needed to cook for hundreds of people but preferred the smaller kitchen when he was only cooking for the royal family and the few invited to share meals at their personal table. It made no sense to Armyn since the man was an alpha and seemed to take up too much space in the little room. He'd caught up to Armyn in three steps and clamped his meaty fist around Armyn's forearm.

"Prince or not, you know you're not allowed in here. And stealing my rolls? Your mother's going to hear about this."

Armyn raised a brow and let a smirk pull up the corner of his lips as he licked icing off them.

"Yeah, at some point Majordomo Meanu will get around to letting Mother know you complained that I stole some rolls. By then, I'll have eaten five more at dinner."

Cook's face flushed a darker shade of purple. Armyn didn't know what species the man was or where he came from, only that he looked a lot like the unbaked lumps of dough resting on the counter, with two sets of beady black eyes mashed in near the top.

"I'll take you to her right now and be sure she bans you from having even one more. You'll learn that you're not above the rules."

Armyn let Cook turn him and drag him to the doorway, shooting a quick glance over his shoulder toward where Cinza hid. His mother likely *would* ban him from having any of the rolls at dinner, but at least he'd saved Cinza from grief. As drawn as he was to pick on her every chance he got, he didn't want her in real trouble. Her reputation of sweet innocence would remain intact.

His mother kept him in her office for hours, making him help her as part of his punishment. She also banned him from having dessert for an entire week, but it wasn't like it would kill him. He still thought it was worth it.

Especially when Cinza pulled him through a doorway into an empty meeting room the day after he'd sacrificed himself for her.

Blood immediately rushed below his belt, and he had to remind himself that this was Cinza. Sweet, innocent, easy to pick on, utterly too naive Cinza. He may have been old enough to have dallied with willing maids, but she was still only fourteen turns.

"What happened? Did you get in trouble?"

Her words were breathy, as if she'd been running or expected him to say he was going to be executed. Chuckling at her worry, he brushed her pale blonde locks over her shoulder.

"No dessert for a week, banned from the kitchens, and I had to help with paperwork. I'll live."

Her eyes seemed to search his face, the tenseness in her body melting away before they narrowed.

"Why did you take the blame? You're no hero. You make my life miserable."

He chuckled again, wings flaring as he shrugged. Reaching out and capturing another lock of her hair, he toyed with the silky strands as he searched for what to say.

"I can't help picking on you. You're so cute when you're angry. But I'm the only one allowed to make you miserable."

He tugged her hair, leaning in close to her ear before continuing.

"I can't have anyone taking my toy away because she got in trouble. Then who would I torture?"

Cinza jerked away, eyes narrowing as he laughed. He wanted to stop her as she moved to stomp past him, but he knew he shouldn't. If anyone caught her in a room alone with him, it would lead to worse punishment than what would have happened if Cook had caught her stealing the roll. It would ruin her reputation.

She stopped in the doorway, turning back to glare at him.

"I was going to say thank you, but I guess I shouldn't since you did it for yourself."

She dug into the satchel hanging across her chest. Pulling something out, she threw it at his face, his hands raising on instinct to catch.

"I made that for you, so you don't have to suffer without dessert."

As she stormed from the room, he looked down at the little package in his hands. Curious, he untied the string holding the paper closed, peeling it back to reveal fresh lemon cookies. His favorite kind.

Grinning, Armyn popped one in his mouth and almost moaned at the explosion of flavor. Cinza may not want to admit it, but the cookies were proof she paid attention to him outside his tormenting of her.

Maybe he'd have to be nice more often.

Chapter 3

Cinza

The library was her safe place. She escaped there when she needed a chance to breathe or relax until her father was ready to head home.

Accepting the stack of books she'd requested from the librarian, Cinza made her way to her favorite table beside the window furthest from the main part of the room. It had become a habit to come there every day after her classes finished. The light came through at the perfect angle, allowing her to read well into the afternoon without blinding her or making her overheat.

It had nothing to do with the fact that the window overlooked the practice yard where

Armyn spent his afternoons in weapons and defense training.

Just the thought of him drew her eyes to the glass, gaze tipping down into the dusty space below. Most of the boys trained in the large yard out past the barns, but Armyn and the other noble boys used the courtyard closest to the guard quarters, since their training was more thorough. Their parents had higher expectations of them, and the captain of the guard himself spent hours training them daily.

Plus, no one wanted to deal with the prince's wounded pride if a commoner somehow struck his precious flesh.

Cinza watched as blue wings flared, catching the sun as Armyn attacked Quasim with his talons. Quasim ducked, rolling away from the slash to lash out with the leading edge of his own wing, knocking Armyn into the dirt before pouncing on his back. She held her breath as she watched; the fight seeming so real she temporarily forgot it was only practice.

Or mostly practice. With the two of them, sometimes it was hard to tell if they were best friends or worst enemies, but in the end, Quasim always gave way to Armyn. It was a little disappointing, if Cinza was honest, since Quasim had the advantage of greater bulk. He apparently also had better restraint.

Pulling her attention back to the books resting in front of her, Cinza flipped the one on top to the section she wanted to read. She'd seen the first of a visiting diplomat's entourage arrive the day before and was curious about their species and home world, since they were so different from the people she was familiar with.

Her focus wavered when someone at a nearby table mentioned Cook was making rolls with the dinner meal. The memory of Armyn catching her stealing a sweet roll two years ago flashed through her mind as clear as though it'd happened yesterday. Her mother didn't allow sweets except for special occasions, and the scent of cinnamon and sugar had entranced Cinza. She hadn't been able to help herself once she saw the fluffy mounds.

A shiver rolled through her body as Cinza remembered Armyn pressing his finger to her sticky lips after startling her. He had brought the finger to his own lips to lick away the sugary sweetness. While the action only confused her then, now it sent a tingle of awareness through her belly.

Glancing out the window again, she watched Quasim's turquoise wings flip through the air before he sprawled on the ground. Armyn extended his hand to help his friend up, reminding

Cinza of an even more confusing time when she'd suffered the prince's attention.

He'd tripped her in the hallway, causing her to land in much the same way as Quasim. When Armyn had offered to help her up, she'd been too scared to take his hand, until he punched Quasim for teasing her. Since that day, she hadn't heard a peep of negativity toward her, but she'd also never found friends. It was as if a bubble separated her from her peers. They were polite if she approached them, but none wanted to get close.

Sighing, Cinza forced her gaze back to the book, but she couldn't help wondering if Armyn had something to do with her inability to fit in with anyone at school. She'd heard him warn Quasim not to be mean to her, but perhaps he'd also told everyone not to be her friend. Her physical differences already isolated her from the other children—she took after her mother's Fayrie side more than her father's Raptyr heritage—but it wouldn't surprise her if Armyn purposefully separated her further from her peers.

Even though she demanded her eyes stay on the book, they shifted to the movement outside the window. Her mouth went dry as Armyn pulled off his shirt, the muscles of his chest rippling in the sunlight. For one insane moment she wondered what it would feel like to run her hands through the little feathers covering his skin, despite—or maybe because of—the way sweat matted them together.

Her wings trembled behind her, refracting sunlight throughout the library.

Armyn had always been the source of her torment, so she didn't know why her thoughts had changed over the last two years. Boys no longer seemed so bad, especially not the older alphas who were closer to being men. Armyn still had two more years before society deemed him an adult and he'd leave for the military, but, compared to the younger boys and even the betas his age, he was far more... developed.

When Cinza looked back down at the notebook under her hand for notes, disgust filled her as she realized little hearts trailed down the side of the page. She shouldn't be having thoughts like that about any boy, much less Armyn. He was not only the Crown Prince, but he was also an ass who liked to pick on smaller, defenseless girls, and her first heat was too far away to use that as an excuse for her wayward thoughts.

A smile pulled at the corners of her lips as she thought about how defenseless Armyn considered her. He'd teased her about it enough times, but she had convinced her father to enroll her in a self-defense course in the city. She'd been studying with them for over a year, and although she hadn't used the training in real life, it was only a matter of time before Armyn cornered her again and she could show him she wasn't as weak and helpless as he thought. He seemed capable of only going so long without hunting her down to tease her, and whether he pushed her in the hall or cornered her in a deserted room, she'd be ready for him.

Gaze drawn back to the irritating male, the smile slipped off Cinza's face as she saw him leaning with one elbow against the wall next to a blushing girl in a maid uniform. The girl ducked her head as if she wasn't enjoying the attention, but Cinza saw her smiles and flirty glances toward the prince. The maid held a basket of towels in front of her for the boys to use, but it was clear from the way Armyn reached out and trailed his fingers across the girl's collarbone that it wasn't the towel he was thinking of using.

Cinza choked off the growl rising in her throat, morphing it into a scoff of disgust as she turned her back to the window and swore she wouldn't look again to see if he left with the girl. Cinza had heard of Armyn's reputation with the maids, but she'd never admit how it made her burn with jealousy to see the truth of it.

The arrogant male could do whatever he wanted. She had more important things to worry about.

And the next time he tried to corner her alone and bully her, she'd quit holding herself back and give him a little surprise of her own.

Chapter 4

Armyn

Holding in a sigh, Armyn kissed the woman's hand before straightening to his full height. The bejeweled and flashy diplomat's wife made him want to roll his eyes and make a cutting remark, but he pasted on his most charming smile and welcomed her to his family's home. The thinly veiled desire shining from the lady's orange irises stroked neither his pride nor his interest.

He wasn't a child anymore. Glittery finery and posh names no longer held his attention. Beautiful women flocked to him his entire life. He'd entertained many needy females over the course of his teen years, but the carefully poised women of his station no longer held his attention.

Neither did the curvy maids or toned garden hands. There was only one female he wanted, but she wasn't ready for him yet.

Cinza.

With her pale flesh and delicate *everything*, there wasn't a single individual in the palace who could compare to her beauty. Some might say she didn't belong in high-class society, but he honestly couldn't think of anyone who displayed more grace or dignity than she did.

In fact, some of her looks in the hall lately had tested his resolve to keep his distance. One haughty yet confusing glance, surrounded by her innocent expression and sweet-looking lips, made his pants shrink and fingers itch to muss her up in every way possible.

He'd refrained for too long.

The little Fayrie was in attendance tonight—all high-class members were required to greet the visiting diplomats and their entourage—but he had yet to see her.

The night was still early. His eagerness to enjoy her expressive eyes and touch her silky flesh made dealing with these pompous oafs more difficult than normal. As soon as they finished introductions and gave an appropriate amount of fawning to the newcomers, Armyn turned to his father and asked for freedom with a raised eyebrow.

Before granting his request, the king turned to Armyn's mother and caressed her arm to gain her attention. Her eyes lit, the epitome of happiness as she smiled up at her mate. Despite his father's age, he still held the stark power of an alpha, yet he coddled his omega the way a big burly male should treat his more fragile female.

Worms wriggled in Armyn's guts as he thought about the way he'd treated his tiny Fayrie when he was younger, but he couldn't change the past. In fact, he wasn't sure he wanted to change his plans for his future actions either.

Something buried deep within his chest begged to know how she'd react if he pushed her a little further.

A little harder.

A little rougher.

He didn't want her to coddle him like everyone else did. He wanted her startled eyes and flushed cheeks to morph into the adorable, mute anger she'd shown the first time he'd pushed her. He wanted the temper she'd given him before flinging sweets she'd baked specially for him at his head.

He wanted the challenge. Needed the bone-deep conviction that the little lady could handle him in all his righteous power.

Spotting the tips of glass-like wings flitting in the room's corner, he knew they belonged to

Cinza. His Tiny was so short, her dainty wings barely topped the shoulders of the other attendees. Armyn waited impatiently for his mother to give her approval for him to step down from the dais.

Although he wanted to launch himself into the air and fly straight to Cinza, he gave a stately bow before stepping down the three stairs when his parents dismissed him. He accepted greetings from those brave enough to approach him, purposefully angling his path toward the wall where Cinza could see him long before he reached her.

Finally getting a clear view of her, he noted the way she gripped her father's arm tighter when she spotted Armyn studying her. After she swallowed, making the delicate column of her throat pulse, she squared her shoulders and lifted one brow. The silent challenge made him glad his current dress coat covered the top half of his thighs. Otherwise, everyone would know how she affected him.

His lips tilted in a smirk as he returned her look, holding her gaze until she glanced away with flushed cheeks.

Armyn turned back into the crowd, slowly drifting closer to the tiny Fayrie and her parents in a meandering path, chatting with friends from school and kissing female hands as was proper.

When he lifted an unmated omega's knuckles to his lips, he fought to hide the kick of discomfort her scent caused him, but seeing Cinza's expression tighten from the corner of his eyes, he made certain she could see every time he touched another woman.

He loved the spark of anger she tried to suppress each time he kissed a hand that belonged to an eligible female, especially the other omegas.

A gentle ping sounded from the speakers hidden around the room, denoting the start of the evening meal, where the highest of royalty and those with invitations to the king's table would depart to the veranda. Most other couples would congregate in the opulent dining hall while the younger attendees enjoyed a more laid-back setting on the lawn between the castle and the garden. The windows of the dining hall overlooked the lawn, which ensured the younger population stayed proper, but during the few minutes of transition, he could speak to his little Fayrie without watchful eyes.

Waiting until her father pecked her on the temple and her mother gave her a gentle hug before they both strode into the crowd to join the group heading to the king's table, Armyn excused himself from the forming group of clingy ladies. The men from his age bracket descended on the dejected girls, giving him a chance to saunter straight for his target.

"Stolen anything from the kitchen lately?"

Wide eyes blinked up at him, her startled expression snapping to annoyance when Cinza realized he was teasing her. The pink tinging her cheeks made her luminescent pale-blue eyes seem more vibrant, but despite her brave facade, her wings fluttered in nervousness and her chest rose and fell as though she'd been running.

"Of course not."

"Maybe you should. Sticky cream looked good on your face."

He chuckled as her pupils shrank in shock. Her cheeks turned a darker pink, the color rising above her neckline to highlight the tantalizing curve of her breasts as her mouth worked in silent fury.

Her body had changed since he'd last approached her, and even though she had more filling out to do before she was ready for him, he couldn't help but appreciate her as she was now.

Her delicate features drew him in most though. They showed every emotion, such as the arousal coursing through her as she bit the inside of her lower lip despite the tightening beside her eyes as she fought anger and nervousness.

"You're disgusting. And I seem to remember you smeared some all over your face too. Maybe you should run around like that more often."

He wanted to throw his head back and roar his laughter but couldn't draw that much attention to them. Instead, he stepped into her space and leaned down, cupping his wings forward so she'd feel surrounded by him.

"If it were *your* cream, I'd happily coat my cheeks with it every day and wear it proudly."

Her bosom heaved as his words sank in, but he didn't relent. Leaning even closer, he dropped his voice and rumbled into her ear.

"I'd fill my mouth with it over and over again, feasting on your sticky sweetness until you begged me to stop. Except I wouldn't."

Armyn shifted closer, forcing her to bend backward as his breath ghosted over her ear.

"You know how I love to torment you, right? I'd lick and suck until you couldn't speak. Nip and sip until you writhed in silent plea. Curl and swirl until you flooded my mouth and filled my belly, then still take more."

He could've murdered himself when he stepped away instead of snatching her up, but he soothed himself by watching the expressions flitting across her face. Her blush could no longer be mistaken for embarrassment or anger—the faint scent of arousal wafted off her skin as she swayed on her feet.

Her mind snapped back into working order with an inaudible pop as her mouth clamped shut, her forehead creasing with confusion.

"Why?"

"Why what?"

"Why are you saying these crude things to me?"

"I'm only telling the truth."

She searched every millimeter of his face before her jaw set in a firm line.

"Is this what you tell every other maiden you hope to bed?"

His finger traced across her cheekbone without his consent, the anger shimmering in her eyes energizing his sadistic heart. He couldn't help the words spilling from his lips even though he was lying. He'd never promised such rapture to anyone else.

"Maybe. What does it matter? It's still true when I say it to you."

Her entire body stiffened, the blush draining away to leave her skin paler than normal. Anger bled from her eyes, leaving behind disappointment so thick it coated his tongue and choked him.

"Leave me alone, Armyn."

She shifted as though to pivot on her heel, but he dropped his hand to her nape and dug his fingertips into the pressure point, keeping his touch much lighter than what he would use to drop a male in battle.

Heated irises flashed to his before she darted her gaze around the room. The second batch of adults chatted as they headed to the dining hall while the youths made use of the brief window of opportunity.

Short of causing a big scene, which would mar her parents' hard-won status and ruin the evening for everyone, she had no choice but to stare up at him and wait for his next move.

"Never," he snarled.

She shrank back but kept her gaze trained on his as he continued.

"I'll never leave you alone. You didn't want my attention so many years ago, yet look at us now. Still playing this game."

His heart stopped in his chest as moisture filled her eyes.

"You were a boy then. It was forgivable. You aren't a boy any longer. Let go, you're hurting me."

She tried to hide her pain, but it vibrated against his fingers. Guilt ballooned in his chest.

He instantly loosened his grip and stroked her shoulder, nearly groaning as he caressed her silky flesh. She raised a hand to wipe an errant tear from her cheek, but he blocked her attempt with his own before brushing it away himself.

The room faded away, her clear blue eyes decimating any pretenses he exuded. His defenses melted, leaving his yearning and weaknesses bared for her to see.

In return, her hopes and dreams shone from her enlarged pupils, her delicate strength knocking his soul into a tailspin. She wanted him, even if she denied it, yet she worried he'd consume her and leave nothing but a broken husk in his wake.

Shaken by the intensity between them, Armyn stepped away, swiping his finger across her cheek one last time before dropping his hands.

He couldn't apologize, even though he knew he should.

"You're right. I'm an alpha. I'll get what I want, no matter what it takes."

Without another word, he turned and walked away, fighting disgust at himself and the roaring lust rushing through his body as the picture of her wide eyes and open-mouthed shock imprinted itself into his memory.

Chapter 5

Cinza

By the time they returned home, Cinza wanted nothing more than to collapse on her bed, but her mother had excused the maid who helped them dress, knowing they wouldn't be home until the middle of the night and wanting the poor girl to sleep well for the next day's tasks. Which left Cinza to help her mother undress from her elaborate gown before she could slip out of her own and escape into sleep.

Only her dreams lately had become less of an escape and more like a strange form of torture. Armyn featured in each one, his powerful body hemming her in as he did things to her no one had ever done.

She shook her head as she plucked another pin from her mother's hair. It seemed like the mass of curls held hundreds of them, and she was so absorbed in the task she startled when her mother spoke.

"Are you and Prince Armyn friends?"

"What?"

Cinza's eyes flashed up to meet her mother's steady gaze in the mirror. Her heart gave a painful lurch as fresh heat swept through her at the delicate raise of a brow.

"No."

Her mouth blurted the word before she thought through her answer, and she had to backtrack to make it sound less harsh when her mother raised a second brow at her.

"I mean, sometimes he talks to me, but I wouldn't call him a friend. We… know each other?"

What she said didn't even make sense to her, so she dropped her gaze back to her mother's hair, hunting for more pins.

"Do you like him?"

The question froze the breath in her lungs. Cinza didn't dare look up and meet her mother's gaze. She did not know what the astute woman would see there.

"N-No. Of course not. He bullies me. He's a spoiled—"

Crushing Cinza

Cinza cut herself off before her mouth completely ran away from her. She was usually better at minding her words, especially with her parents, but after what Armyn had done to her at the reception, he was a sore subject.

"He knows he can get away with it," she finished.

Her mother's chuckle surprised her, and she couldn't stop herself from looking up into the mirror again. Her mother's blue eyes, so much like her own, sparkled with mirth as she tried to suppress a smile.

Feeling her forehead crinkle in irritation, Cinza looked away and went back to her task, the last pin coming free of her mother's hair and sending the golden locks cascading down her back. Hand raising to take hers, her mother turned around. Cinza had no way to hide her expression.

"Darling, you know boys only pick on girls they like."

She graced her daughter with a soft smile as she patted her hand.

"I'll admit, it's not the brightest plan, but it gets our attention. They eventually grow out of it, but it can take a while for some of them."

Patting her hand again, her mother released her and stood as Cinza stared, dumbfounded. Armyn had made plenty of innuendos over the last couple years, but she'd never taken him seriously, even if he made her burn with confused desire. If anything, she only thought he wanted to mount her like he did everything else that walked.

Yet as that thought passed through her head, she realized she hadn't heard of any new rumors about him in quite some time. Females still flocked to the practice yard where he spent his afternoons, but the other boys seemed to show them more attention than Armyn did. She hadn't noticed him give any girl the special attention he had in his youth.

Confusion churned inside her. She was still furious about what he'd said to her before dinner, and he'd danced with every female besides her when the music began, yet some stupid spark of hope flared at her mother's words, latching onto them in a wild dream that they were true.

Armyn had never said he liked her. He'd done nothing to make her think she was more than another easy target.

Yet he had always seemed to pay more attention to her than anyone else. Even if that attention was mostly negative, there were a few moments where he'd been surprisingly kind.

Cinza shook her head, reaching for the laces of her mother's gown to give herself something to do as she tried to calm her thoughts.

"Armyn isn't interested in anything besides making things as difficult as possible for me. Plus, he's older than me, and the Crown Prince. He'll match with some fancy princess or a high-ranking official's daughter."

"He's only a couple of years older, and *you* are a high-ranking official's daughter."

Her mother turned and gave her a pointed stare, which Cinza ignored. She didn't fit in with the other high-class females her age, so she didn't see herself as eligible for the title. She doubted anyone else did either. Her father had earned everyone's respect, but Cinza had only ever been a shadow in his wake. She doubted the king and queen would even consider her as a match since she had nothing to offer the crown.

When she remained silent, her mother sighed and turned to face her once again. Gripping Cinza's arms, she forced Cinza to meet her gaze.

"Your life is up to you. I'm just saying to keep an open mind. I saw how he watched you tonight, and it wasn't the gaze of a male who didn't care. He wanted a reaction."

One hand moved from Cinza's arm to cup her chin.

"I know there are no available princesses of proper age within our galaxy. Your father has known the king for longer than he's been an advisor, and I don't think the match would be impossible if that was what you wanted."

Chapter 6

Armyn

He knew he'd find her in the library, but the sight of Cinza trailing a finger down the edge of a book while she stared out the window nearly short-circuited his brain. He stood frozen, studying her features and soaking in her presence. Her wings pulsed behind her, the unconscious motion small and slow as her mind wandered.

Armyn's attention narrowed to her face, the scrunch of her brows and downward curve of her lips causing concern to wriggle into his guts.

Someone so delicate and beautiful shouldn't look so melancholy, but a grin stole onto his face as he noted her scent. A slight flush crept up her bosom. Whatever she'd been considering left residual arousal.

Was she thinking of him? Was she sad he was leaving?

Yesterday his father had announced Armyn's military departure date. Armyn had been preparing for his time in the service his entire life—every leader within his future kingdom was required to have military experience in their background. He was looking forward to his time of adventure and independence from his royal duties.

But it appeared his little Fayrie was not, which made him happy because it meant she cared.

Stalking across the nearly deserted room on silent talons, Armyn enjoyed Cinza's quiet squeak of alarm when he snuck up behind her and leaned over her. After pressing his palm onto the desk beside the book she ignored, he hummed his pleasure as he dragged her scent deeper into his lungs.

"That's a pretty sound."

"Y-you're such a jerk. Get away from me."

"You're so ready to see me go you'd ruin a perfectly splendid opportunity to give me a proper goodbye?"

She stiffened under him, her wings fluttering against his chest before going statue still.

"Why are you bothering me?"

"I leave tomorrow. I couldn't go without making sure you knew the score."

"There's a score now? First, you bully me every chance you get. Then you say dirty things and claim you'll do anything to get me to like you. Now you're giving me an ultimatum before disappearing for years?"

"Hush, Tiny."

She sucked in a breath as he ducked his head so close his breath ghosted over her ear.

"First, I said nothing about you liking me. I said I'd do anything to have you, which still stands. Second, I'm not giving you an ultimatum, only helping you realize the truth."

Her words were barely audible even with his excellent hearing, the tremors making her whisper uneven.

"And what's the truth?"

He brushed the edge of her ear with his lips, enjoying her gasp before he spoke again.

"You're free to do as you please while I'm gone. I don't care."

Those words killed him to say. He cared. Far too much. But he had to give her the illusion of an option. There was nothing he could do while he wasn't present, so he had to convince himself he didn't care what happened.

"But when I get back?"

He stood and stepped around her so his thigh brushed her shoulder and his crossed arms made her lean to avoid him.

"You're mine. At least for a little while."

Her cheeks flamed a bright red as her eyes flashed with anger.

"And if I have a mate?"

"You won't."

Her mouth popped open, the stunned rage on her face obvious as she jumped to her feet on the other side of the chair before he uncrossed his arms.

"You'll be gone for six years. Six years, Armyn!"

He lifted a brow as her tiny hands curled into fists at her sides.

"Are you saying I'm so ugly no one else will want me? Or do you mean you've already warned all the alphas away from me?"

He almost stepped back in shock at the hurt filling her eyes, her voice thick with the tears she refused to shed. While he *had* told his peers he'd castrate any male who tried to gain her favor, he hadn't meant for it to warp the way she saw herself. He hadn't meant to make her feel unwanted or undeserving, yet the agony threatening to drip from her lashes told him he'd done exactly that.

Forgetting the chair was between them, he stepped forward, only to lose his balance as the unexpected barrier knocked into her. She squeaked and pinwheeled her arms. Time slowed as adrenaline lit his senses. He reached out for her, his stomach jolting into his throat in a way he hadn't felt since he'd first learned to fly, but she righted herself by flitting her wings and sticking a foot behind her.

She swatted his seeking hands with surprising force. His brows popped up as she planted her feet and sent her tiny fist toward his throat.

Mesmerized by the concentrated, fierce expression in her eyes, he didn't even think of dodging.

If he'd been a lesser alpha or a beta, her jab would have sent him dropping to the floor in agony. Instead, he caught her wrist during the follow-through and growled as pain streaked up and down his throat.

She yanked on her arm, but he refused to let go. He jerked her tiny body toward him. She hissed as her thighs collided with the chair. His hackles rose and growl deepened.

"So the tiny Fayrie took defense classes. I'm amused you thought you could hurt me but am happy you think of me so much."

Her pupils shrank as she stilled, his rumble rushing through her nerves.

"Let go of me."

Armyn sighed, exaggerating the sound so he could watch Cinza's eyes widen.

"I told you already. Never."

Her jaw tightened before she tried to pull her wrist out of his hold.

"Go ahead, Cinza. Keep fighting me. Keep telling me no. When I get back, you'll welcome me with open arms."

She stopped her frantic jerking, meeting his stare with a challenge of her own.

"Oh? And why is that?"

"Because you'll never find an alpha with my strength. No one will know you better than I. No one will pleasure you as well as I can."

Cinza's chest heaved as she grit her teeth. Her annoyance and denial irked Armyn so much he lost his control. He flung the chair out of the way and plastered their fronts together. Pulling her wrist behind his back, he forced her to stay against him while he pivoted and backed her against the edge of the table.

"Just once, before I go."

Armyn lowered his head and filled his fist with the hair near her scalp, holding Cinza in place while he invaded her mouth. Hot and decadent, she tasted sweeter than the rolls she'd stolen so many years ago. He took what he knew he shouldn't, too enthralled as she melted under him, her shock giving way to submission.

As he stroked his tongue along hers, she responded with a tentative twitch.

He cursed himself. This was probably her first kiss, yet he was nearly shoving his tongue down her throat and showing her just how crazy she made him. Armyn gentled his ministrations, coaxing her to respond instead of demanding she accept whatever he gave her.

Ever so slowly, she roused, her pert breasts rubbing against him as he released her locks and wrapped his digits around her nape instead.

Her sweet scent thickened as she came alive under his mouth until he burned so hot for her he worried the flames would scorch his wings and he'd never be able to fly except with her in his arms.

Pulling away, he nipped her bottom lip before devoting her delighted, dazed face to his memory.

He stepped away, knowing if he touched her again he'd never be able to stop himself despite her body not being ready for him. Her expression morphed into one of confusion.

"Remember that when you're trying to find another male, and know without a doubt, he'll never compare. I'll be back, Cinza."

He took another step away without looking, awareness of their surroundings seeping in for the first time since he'd approached her. The few people in the room made little sound besides their breathing, no doubt cataloging every moment to feed the rumor mills.

"You'd better be ready for more when I return. You're mine."

His chest ached as he turned from her, and his mind rebelled as he put distance between them. He wanted to turn around and beg her to wait for him. He wanted to demand she think of him and only him. He wanted her everything—her first heat, her claiming, her fierceness and devotion—but he forced his feet onward without looking back.

She wouldn't believe him if he told her, and even if she did, there was no way for him to stay.

He had an obligation to his people, responsibilities to fulfill, and duties to uphold. He could not promise her those things then desert her.

But maybe his kiss would endear him to her while he was away.

His next six years seemed to stretch before him into infinity.

He couldn't wait to get back.

Chapter 7

Cinza

"A ball?"

Cinza resisted the urge to turn up her nose at her mother's announcement. With the way she felt, going to a ball was the last thing she wanted to do.

"Yes! It's a bit of a costume ball. You're supposed to wear gowns from other cultures. It'll be so fun. I have the perfect dress for you in storage. It was one of my mother's from her time on Fayrier."

Sighing, Cinza resigned herself to going along with her mother. It wasn't like she could refuse, though claiming to be ill was a temptation she nearly accepted. She'd certainly felt ill the past few weeks since Armyn left.

Turning her thoughts away from the missing male, she pasted a smile on her face. She was *not* moping because he'd left, merely worrying about all the other classmates who'd left in the same wave of recruitment and what could happen to her kingdom if the prince failed to return.

Her mother was so excited she insisted they immediately go to the attic and forage through the old trunks stored there. Many of them had come with her to Allhert when she married Cinza's father and had remained closed since before Cinza was born.

Their housekeeper of only six days accompanied them. Her mother hadn't planned to change maids, but when their long-term, deeply trusted servant had serious medical issues giving birth to twins, she had unhappily accepted the woman's announcement that she wouldn't return. Cinza still wasn't comfortable with the new housekeeper, uncertain about the expressions flashing across her face when she thought no one was looking. Cinza's wings fluttered with the sense of unease crawling up her spine, unsure if she'd seen the female giving the back of her mother's head a sour look or if that was just her unhappiness at having to climb the stairs.

Looking around the crowded space of the attic, her mother didn't seem to notice the housekeeper's surliness, which only seemed to get worse with each trunk Mother requested she open. Cinza wrestled up the lid of one of the ornate boxes herself, but the massive thing was heavier than it looked, with wicked prongs extending from the locking mechanism that made her leery to try another.

It took a while before her mother exclaimed and knelt in front of the most recently opened trunk. Glistening wings fluttering in her excitement, she pulled out the folded gowns stacked inside.

Cinza let out an audible gasp at the gorgeous dresses, the color of the fabric still vibrant despite the years locked away. Vivid reds and jewel greens puddled around her mother's slim frame, but her attention caught on a deep blue.

"This one. This one is perfect for you," her mother said as she shook out the gown.

Cinza's fingers trembled as she reached to take the dress from her mother's outstretched hands. The fabric was soft, the entire gown lighter than she'd expected, with the layers that cascaded down the skirt. Holding it to her chest, she marveled at the exotic cut.

"It's beautiful!"

Cinza couldn't help the smile pulling up her cheeks, excitement building in her chest at the prospect of getting to wear the gorgeous gown.

"There are shoes and jewelry to go with it in here too."

Her mother leaned over the side of the trunk, digging into the bottom in search of the accessories. Looking down at the dress held to her front, Cinza smoothed out the skirt and twirled, giggling until a sudden bang caused her to jump.

Eyes darting over her shoulder to where her mother had knelt beside the trunk, her mind stuttered at what she saw. For a long, indeterminate moment, nothing made sense. The lid of the trunk her mother had pulled her gorgeous dress from had fallen partially closed, and something glossy stuck out the edges, quivering with the force of the slam.

Dawning horror stole her breath as Cinza noticed her mother's pink dress wedged beneath the glossy material, and her heart stumbled as she made the connection that it wasn't fabric fluttering—those were her mother's wings.

Rushing to the side of the trunk, Cinza fell to her knees with a cry, the blue gown forgotten on the floor. She struggled to lift the lid, but the trunk was larger than the one she'd opened before, and she had to fight to lever it off her mother's back.

Cinza's hands flew to her mouth when the lid rocked open. Her mother didn't move. Spine and wings limp, arms and head hanging into the deep chest, her back didn't rise or fall with breath.

Eyes swimming with tears, her arms extended in slow motion. Reaching over her mother's back, Cinza gripped her slim shoulders.

"Mom?"

The word was a shaky whisper that got no response. A scuff beside her jerked Cinza's head to the side, the housekeeper's form wavering into view as tears finally spilled down Cinza's cheeks.

"You bumped the lid when you spun. The prongs of the lock… She was leaning right over them. She's dead."

The woman's words were the last thing Cinza knew before she slid into darkness.

***

Cinza didn't know how much time had passed since her mother's funeral. Excused from the last of her classes, there was nothing to differentiate between one day and the next, only a constant aching hole in her chest.

But the waves of heat followed by sweats that left her chilled were new. Sensations crawled along her flesh, leaving her feeling itchy and restless, but she accepted the thought of being ill as punishment for what she'd done.

"You need to take these."

The housekeeper pressed something into her palm, holding out a glass of water. Cinza uncurled her fingers to see two tiny red pills. She almost rejected them, sure she deserved to suffer, but words escaped her cracked lips before she could stop them.

"What are they?"

Her voice was a whispered croak, weeks of silence and sobbing making it seem insubstantial. She could feel the bones in her shoulder shifting as she accepted the water, the lack of eating more than a couple bites at a time for so long having diminished what little cushion she'd built before her world crumbled.

"You're going into heat. I can smell the scent of it on you. Those are suppressants. They'll stop it if you take them in time."

Cinza didn't care about the way the housekeeper's nose scrunched and lips curled in disgust at the mention of heat. As a beta, the woman likely found an omega's cycle disturbing, and Cinza couldn't blame her. She hadn't gone through one herself yet, but her mother had described it, and her cycle wasn't something she wanted to deal with in her current state.

The thought of her mother brought fresh tears to her eyes. Popping the little pills into her mouth, Cinza sucked down the water before collapsing back onto her pillow and letting her eyes close.

Her fault.

It was her fault her mother was gone. No matter how many times her father tried to assure her of her innocence after she'd confessed her part in the accident, Cinza knew the truth. She could see it in the disgusted housekeeper's eyes.

***

Another month or more passed before her father came into her room early one morning. Rubbing the sleep from her eyes, Cinza forced herself to sit up, unsure what could have brought him when he hadn't bothered to come before. He'd left her to her grief, the weight of his own leaving no strength to carry hers as well.

"I'm leaving."

His abrupt announcement jerked Cinza to full awareness. Scrambling from her bed, she tried to smooth her rumpled nightdress as she stumbled closer to him near the foot of her bed.

"But... I..."

Her father's gaze dragged over her before focusing on a point above her head.

"I've accepted an assignment to travel to Treag Prime to negotiate a new trade contract for the king. I'll likely be gone a few weeks. Eevid will be here to look after you."

Her father had never traveled before, so Cinza didn't understand why he was suddenly leaving. Her mind latched onto the one thing she could make sense of in the face of his news.

"Who's Eevid?"

"The housekeeper. You really should know the name of the person who's been taking care of you, Cinza."

Her father's stern eyes dropped to hers but wavered in her view as Cinza's eyes flooded. Her father had tried to comfort her after the accident, but he'd had his own grief to bear as well and had withdrawn shortly after the funeral. Now he seemed... cold, and she felt more alone than ever.

"I-I'm sorry. I can do better. Please stay!"

The thought of her father leaving had her fighting back sobs that threatened to rip her to pieces. She knew the distance between them was her fault since she'd stayed in her room wallowing in grief. But how could she correct that if he wasn't there?

"I've already decided. I leave in a few hours."

Her wings drooped as her shoulders curled around the aching gash in her chest. Expression softening, her father closed the space between them and pulled her into his arms.

"I hate seeing you like this. I know it's hard, but... you've got to pull yourself out of it. And I need to get away for a bit. I need to go somewhere that doesn't hold so many memories of her."

Sniffling, Cinza nodded, slipping a hand up to wipe her face as her father released her and stepped back. It wasn't fair of her to demand he stay if traveling would help him heal. Perhaps she could find a little healing herself while he was gone.

"The preliminary agreement is done, so it shouldn't take more than a few weeks to travel there, finalize everything, and come home. Once I'm back, we can sit down and have dinner together."

Cinza nodded again, sucking in a deep breath to fortify herself. Her father was right, she couldn't wallow in her misery forever. She had to get through this, even if it was only one day at a time.

"That sounds nice," she whispered.

Her eyes focused on his wings as he turned to walk away. He held them erect and stiff, trying to hide the pain she knew he still carried, and there was something about them that made her think of Armyn.

He shut the door between them before she had the chance to say goodbye. Head dropping, her gaze moved over the state of her clothing, her nose twitching as she noticed the scent rising from her for the first time. If she was going to make any progress moving past her trauma, she figured she could start with a bath. From there, perhaps she could find the will to clean her room, and after that… She'd take things one task at a time.

***

"I have something I'd like to tell you."

Cinza looked up from the plate in front of her, meeting her father's eyes across the table. He'd kept his promise to have dinner with her after he'd returned, and they'd continued to eat together each night for the past two weeks. She still found it hard to stomach much, but the few bites she was managing at each meal had brought back a bit more of her energy.

She'd also started leaving her room more often, finding chores around the house to keep her occupied. It started with little things here and there, but she'd progressed to helping with each meal, and it made her feel like she was accomplishing something useful for the first time in months.

"Yes?"

Her thoughts tumbled over each other as she wondered what would cause her father to sound so formal. They usually tried to make small talk before their meal began, but they spent the rest of their time in silence as they ate.

Eevid stepped up behind her father's wing, drawing Cinza's gaze. The smirk on the woman's lips was odd, but Cinza shook off the weird clenching in her stomach and pulled her attention back to her father.

"I know this may seem sudden, and I assure you it's not meant to slight your mother, but I'm marrying Eevid."

One small hand lifted to lie on her father's shoulder. Eevid's slimy smile spread as Cinza's jaw fell open. All she could do was stare, eyes jerking between her father's blank expression and the housekeeper's oily satisfaction. Her mouth worked, but her brain stumbled over words, unable to put any in an order that encompassed the way she felt.

Her father continued in her silence.

"It's a matter of convenience, but you'll still show her the respect she deserves. You need someone to watch over you, and I'm going to be away more often handling negotiations. Eevid has stepped up and shown herself caring and capable since your mother's—"

He paused and sucked in a harsh breath that Cinza echoed before continuing.

"Since we hired her. I'm leaving again in three weeks, so we're going to have the wedding the weekend after next. I know it's fast, but we only need something small."

The news that the wedding was happening so soon was a blow to the gut, and the knowledge that her father was leaving again right after stole what little breath Cinza had left. The only spark of satisfaction came from the way Eevid's expression slipped at her father's declaration that the ceremony would be small.

Fists clenching in her lap, only the scrape of her nails along trembling flesh kept Cinza centered. She pinched her lips, chest heaving, knowing nothing she said would matter. Her father wasn't the type to be talked out of something after he'd decided, and any resistance from her would only make things worse.

Swallowing, she sucked in a breath and straightened her shoulders.

"May I be excused?"

Tiny lines appeared around her father's eyes, but he gave her a nod. Eevid was more open with her glare as Cinza stood to leave. Turning to flee from the room before her emotions exploded and drove a further wedge between her and her father, Cinza stopped when Eevid made one last announcement.

"We'll move my daughter into the house in a few days. I'm sure you won't mind helping her choose a room and settle in."

The voice behind her sounded nothing like the blunt tones Eevid had always used with Cinza. Sickeningly sweet, the honeyed words were still clearly an order, not a question.

Looking back over her shoulder, Cinza tried and failed to force a smile on her face.

"Of course."

Cinza recognized the spark in Eevid's eyes for what it was, and her wounded heart dropped further. It hadn't seemed like her life could get any worse, but the promise on the former housekeeper's face was clear. Nothing was going to get better.

Chapter 8

Armyn

Armyn dropped his gear next to the decrepit cot and shook his head.

"Why are we always getting the crappy barracks?"

Silence met him as his teammates began their evening routine. Quasim tossed a few items from the top of his pack onto his bed before shaking out his wings and sitting down. Blaide dropped his stuff beside the head of his cot and plopped himself onto the bare mattress, sliding a knife from its holster and sharpening the already deadly weapon. Ursuli shook his head and started cleaning his area with flicks of his smoke. When the light of the single bare bulb reflected off the metal of the cot and the surface of the tiny table beside it, Armyn sighed and turned to look at his own temporary resting place.

"Why do you bother to clean, anyway? It's not like you actually touch it while you sleep."

Ursuli, the medic of his team, merely sent him a side glare before bending to open his pack. He kept himself solid most of the time, but sometimes while his mind recharged at night he slipped and sent his body into his incorporeal form. The first time Armyn had seen the cloud of inky blackness floating above the cot where Ursuli should have been lying had terrified him.

Quasim snorted and ran his fingers down the ruffled feathers of his wings. The mission they'd completed mere hours ago had been a week-long endeavor behind enemy lines, with little chance of grooming. They all looked a bit ragged.

Armyn wondered how Cinza would react if she saw him as he was now—grubby from hiding in whatever unoccupied hovel they could find and wearing clothes he'd had to wash with minimal water. He didn't look kingly, but his square jaw and sharp cheekbones now held an air of menace he couldn't hide. He'd looked much worse over the years, but although his memories of her crept in whenever his guard was down, he'd done his best to keep his focus on the present.

"Hey, at least we don't have to sleep with our backs together in some ditch somewhere.

Although I *will* miss Blaide's soft, cuddly tail," Quasim rumbled.

He chuckled when Blaide hissed and flung a knife toward him. Catching it with ease, Quasim tossed it into the air and caught it with his other hand before he sent it back toward Blaide.

Blaide snatched it out of the air and laughed, his naturally laid-back personality returning now that his knife had avenged the ribbing about his tail. The Vuk was proud of the fluffy thing, spending more time grooming it than he did the rest of his body. Armyn and their other teammates couldn't help but tease him regularly about it.

"How long have we been at this, grouch? You still can't get over how amazing my tail is? The ladies can't either, so…"

Ursuli rolled his eyes while Quasim snorted, and Armyn shook his head. With his deep baritone voice soft yet serious, Ursuli sat up and braced his knees on his elbows.

"Almost five years. We've been on covert ops for almost five years."

He studied his interlocked fingers before looking at each of the males within the tent.

"I've served for longer than I care to admit. I'm here for this team, but…"

Dread built in Armyn's chest. He'd grown to love these men, each one having saved his life many times over the years, much as he had saved theirs, and parting would surely destroy the last bits of levity in his soul. They'd seen terrible things together, survived horrible situations, and yet together they still felt whole and as normal as could be.

If Ursuli was ready to end his time in the service, then where did that leave the rest of them?

Armyn and Quasim had about ten months left before their contracts ended. Would Ursuli extend his time until then, or would they have to suffer missions without his life-saving talents? How would they survive without the best surgeon in the Empyre to hold them together when things went sour?

"I'm tired of the death and all the shit they put us through. I'll stick around for this team, even re-enlist on a charter contract until we all decide we're done, but I just feel stretched too thin. Each new attack, every death, every patient I have to treat or leave to suffer… it all drains me so much more than it used to."

The room fell silent except for the wind buffeting the fabric of the tent, each of his teammates letting Ursuli's words sink in. Armyn studied the oldest member of their unit and saw the strain in his glowing pink orbs and the droop of his shoulders. Ursuli clearly hated giving them the news, but after their last grueling mission, Armyn understood.

Blaide broke the silence in his usual snarky fashion.

"That's good, old man. My time is up in about six months—you can hold on until then. Nobody cares about the Raptyrs anyway. Their feathers are worth less than fletching."

Quasim snorted again, going back to smoothing his wing as he shook his head.

The dread growing in Armyn's guts didn't relent. He searched his brothers' faces and noted their pensive expressions, despite their attempts to camouflage them.

Every time anything went wrong on a mission, they each responded with swift, direct actions. He couldn't let this worry fester between them.

"No matter what happens, we're brothers. Even when we finish slogging through shitholes and no longer have to worry about getting shot at by scum, we'll still have each other's backs."

"Duh. That's what brothers do," Blaide said, as though any of them had been born with siblings. Quasim rolled his eyes but nodded his agreement. Ursuli grunted his acknowledgment before settling back onto his cot.

Yet the worry building in Armyn's chest didn't lessen.

Thinking of the lonely nights when all he'd had were his memories of pale flesh and luminescent blue eyes, he wanted excitement to course through him as he contemplated the end of his contract. With his six years nearly complete, he should prepare to woo the female who'd snuck past his defenses as a teen, but the dread behind his sternum blocked it.

All four of them shot to their feet, talons, or paws as boots thundered closer to their tent. When a courier burst through the opening and skidded to a halt, the already toxic premonition building inside Armyn's ribcage burst to catastrophic levels. The skinny beta swung his eyes around the room before thrusting the missive clutched tightly in his hand to Armyn.

"Urgent," was all the male said before he pivoted on his heel and ran back into the elements.

"Fuck, not even a full day since we got back on this side of the barrier!"

Blaide's curse barely registered through the thick dread stuffing Armyn's ears. He ignored the ridiculous emotion and put his body into motion, slicing open the envelope and reading it aloud. He'd never treated his team as anything but equals, even though technically he was in charge, so keeping the new information from them by reading it to himself would be foolhardy.

"Look at it this way, fluffy butt. At least we don't have to pack up before we leave," Quasim snarled as he tossed the few things he'd taken out back into the top of his pack.

In a matter of seconds, Armyn led his brothers out of yet another broken promise of hot food and decent rest, back toward enemy lines.

Despite having completed innumerable covert ops, Armyn couldn't shake the nasty trepidation clinging to his insides. Something felt wrong this time around, but he had no concrete evidence of why, so he did what had kept them alive for the past five years.

He closed off his emotions and pushed forward, trusting his teammates with his life and promising to protect theirs no matter the cost.

If only he'd voiced his concerns, maybe things would have worked out differently. Instead, he'd kept his mouth shut and built his own cage of grief.

***

Armyn blinked and tried to force himself to focus on his mother's face. She looked beautiful, as always, yet he couldn't keep his mind from shorting out and slipping back into the past.

Since returning home yesterday, his brain refused to compute his sudden change of environment. After years of crawling through dirt and living a heartbeat away from death, the shiny opulence and ridiculous pompousness he found himself in made no sense.

This no longer felt like his life, his time in the military seeming more real. He'd grown up here yet never noticed how fake everything was.

Except it wasn't fake. His mother wasn't fake. Her eyebrows were scrunched, her worry for him clear in the way she stared at him. He knew her responsibilities were very real, understood how much worse the world could be if people didn't rule with fairness, but he couldn't muster up the courage to deal with her concern.

"Of course, Mother. With you in charge, my homecoming ball will be magnificent. I trust you to make the best choices. If you'll excuse me, please?"

"Armyn, look at me."

He gritted his teeth and swallowed as he met his mother's kind gaze.

"Your father had trouble when he returned as well. He found help. I hope you will too if you decide you need it."

After murmuring his thanks and kissing her knuckles, he stalked out the door. His talons carried him toward his private rooms, but disgust turned him down a side hall. The thought of pounding his fists into someone's flesh held appeal, but he'd never trust himself with anyone other than the friend he'd grown up sparring with.

Quasim's absence was worse than a knife in his side. His best friend and beloved teammate hadn't been fit for duty after their last mission went south, so after a few months of surgeries and physical therapy, their command medically discharged him. Armyn was glad Quasim hadn't had to stick around to see the sad side of the military—Armyn hated the administrative tasks and lazy personnel who never saw the field—but he wished he could have come home with his most trusted partner-in-crime at his side. His stomach had dropped when he stepped off the ship and found his friend wasn't even in the capital.

Nothing was okay anymore. He'd fucked up and gotten his team captured. They'd been prisoners of the enemy for four days before rescue reached them, except the rescue team hadn't found Quasim.

The enemy had tortured him. Taken something he'd never get back, permanently damaging the powerful alpha and scarring their medic when he barely kept Quasim alive.

His best friend wasn't the same anymore because Armyn hadn't warned them. His instincts had told him something was wrong, but he'd ignored the feeling and pushed on, too sure of their prowess to open his mouth and admit he was worried.

Armyn turned down another hallway, not caring where he ended up so long as he found fresh air and solitude. For such a massive castle, there weren't many places to be alone. Even his own rooms weren't safe with the bevy of servants constantly in and out.

He blindly turned another corner. A feminine squeak bounced off the walls as a tiny body ricocheted off his front. He snatched the female's shoulders to stop her from falling but released the bony joints the second she regained her balance.

His mouth dried and the apology on his tongue morphed to sandpaper when he looked down at the female he'd crashed into.

Cinza's blue irises stood out amid her pale beauty, the orbs seeming much larger than he remembered. The roundness of youth no longer remained in her face, replaced by even sweeter angles and more fragile features than the ones etched in his memory.

Mute anger gripped him, his senses shutting down instead of exploding at the unfairness of her timing. Tomorrow evening at his homecoming ball, he'd have his thoughts tucked away and his princely mask on, but now?

Now he was nothing but a seething ball of rage and misery, lost in the dark memories of his past and the uncertainty of his future. And here she was, the reality of the ghost who'd haunted him the past six years, more tempting than the picture he'd cherished all that time.

"H-hi, Armyn. I heard you'd returned. I—"

His guts tightened as her delight dimmed, the shock of happiness in her eyes draining away as she studied his face. He'd wanted her and Quasim to be there when he'd disembarked, but he had given them the benefit of the doubt—maybe they hadn't known when he'd returned. Her words proved him wrong.

"What are you doing here?"

He didn't mean to growl or sound so disgusted, but he couldn't reconcile his gruesome memories with the sparkling beauty in front of him.

"Oh, um, I'm taking a letter to my father."

Alarm bells rang in his head, so distant he didn't recognize them through his fury as his subconscious noted her stance. With shoulders rolled forward and her eyes darting around the hallway, she lacked the fierceness he remembered lurking in her depths. Fear emanated from her, but he refused to acknowledge he was the reason for it.

"It—it's good to see you," she whispered, almost as though she was ashamed to say the words aloud.

Armyn scoffed. The last time they'd interacted, she'd basically said she never wanted to see him again.

"Sure. It's great to be back, even though no one bothered to greet me except my parents."

Cinza's shoulders dipped deeper into their curl at his bland words. Whatever hope she'd held drained from her expression as he watched.

Shit, he was fucking up even more.

"I haven't seen Quasim. Is he back too?"

How had she found the one thing he would detonate over? She hadn't attempted to welcome him home but asked about another alpha?

Armyn's fog disappeared with a clap of thunder, except the sound came from his chest. His growl shamed him further, even as he severed whatever else may have lingered between them.

"For someone who thought six years was a long time, you sure haven't matured a goddamn bit. Take your pathetic eyes and fake greetings where they're wanted because I can't stand them for another second."

Refusing to look away as his words struck her, he watched in abject horror as she morphed into a breathing shell. All emotion leaked out of her expression until she stood as empty as the women he'd saved from years of abuse.

Without another sound, she tucked the paper to her chest and ducked her chin before stepping around him. He'd extinguished the spark in her eyes. The fierceness he'd coveted for years no longer existed.

Guilt buried him until the only thing he could do was remain silent and move his body.

He proved how much of a coward he was by walking away.

Chapter 9

Cinza

She shut down the pain the same way she'd buried the grief of her mother's death—by refusing to feel. Letting everything drain through her as if she had holes in her feet, Cinza stepped around Armyn and continued down the hall without a backward glance.

It didn't matter that each breath ladened with his pheromones felt like shards of glass piercing her lungs. The last six years had been one disappointment after another, so why had she held onto the hope that seeing Armyn again would be any different?

Her eyes stung because of the bright light in the halls and nothing more.

She tapped on the door of her father's office, waiting for permission to enter. The tired smile he sent her when he looked up and realized it was her who knocked helped ease some of the pressure on her chest.

"Eevid wanted me to bring this to you."

She extended the envelope across the desk, folding her hands in front of her as she waited for his response. It wasn't the first time her stepmother sent her to her father with a message deemed of the utmost importance, and Cinza knew better than to leave before her father gave an answer.

He scanned the message before rubbing his temples with one hand. He'd only been home from his latest trip for two days, and he looked like he hadn't slept the entire time.

Pulling open the drawer next to him, he dug into it before taking out a handful of bills to stuff into the envelope. While many people kept their credits stored with finance institutions and used their cards to cover costs, her father had always been old-fashioned and kept the bulk of his wealth in paper currency.

"That's all I have right now. That should be enough for three dresses."

He handed the envelope back as Cinza's breath stuttered.

"Dresses?"

Eevid hadn't said what the message was about, but that was nothing new to Cinza. The woman barely acknowledged her unless she was giving orders.

"Your stepmother wants the three of you to have new dresses for the prince's homecoming ball. I thought she just bought new dresses, but I guess those aren't the right kind."

He rubbed his forehead again, leaving the small downy feathers ruffled. Cinza realized they were thinning around his eyes, showing his age and the stress he'd been under, and a fresh pang stabbed through her chest.

Despite being an adult, her mother's death had knocked Cinza's life off course, and she still lived with and relied on her father for support. She'd been so busy she hadn't had time to consider what she would do if it ended.

Saying goodbye to her father, Cinza left the palace and made her way home. When her mother had been alive, they'd lived in a comfortable house tucked away on the other side of the wall near the palace gardens, but it hadn't been good enough for Eevid. She'd wanted something newer, closer to the center of the town and the shops she frequented, and Cinza suspected her father agreed to the move to escape the ghost of her mother's memories.

The new house had cost quite a bit, and since Eevid insisted on replacing all the furniture as well, they'd had to cut expenses in other areas. They could no longer afford the salary of a housekeeper, and as the new bride, Eevid had refused to continue performing the duty. Her daughter, Goziva, seemed perfectly content to live in her own filth, so it fell to Cinza to keep the house clean and meals ready.

Pausing with her hand on the doorknob, Cinza sucked in a deep breath to prepare herself. The walk to and from the palace had been the closest she'd come to having a break in too long.

She cracked open the back door, the oiled hinges moving silently as she slipped inside and closed it behind her. Thinking she'd have a moment to make herself some lunch before letting Eevid know she'd returned, Cinza winced as a sharp voice called from the doorway.

"It's about time you returned. I told you not to dawdle."

Smoothing her expression, she ducked her head and turned to face her stepmother.

"I'm sorry."

It didn't matter that she'd walked as fast as she could or that there had been a line to get through the gate. Eevid didn't accept excuses.

Heels clicked across the tiled floor, the shiny points stopping in front of Cinza as she kept her gaze on the floor. A demanding hand extended into view, red nails meticulously filed into points that reminded Cinza of claws.

Removing the envelope of money from her pocket, she passed it into Eevid's waiting hand. It was mere seconds before the first complaint began.

"This isn't enough for three ballgowns! Does he expect us to wear last year's dresses from some bargain store?"

Cinza knew Eevid wasn't looking for an answer from her. Nothing she said would matter and would likely only earn her extra chores. The woman just liked to complain.

"We're going to be laughed out of the ball. This is Goziva's only chance at a first impression. She must have the best."

Glossy shoes turned, heels tapping an angry tattoo across the floor as Eevid left the kitchen. Cinza's shoulders relaxed from beside her ears, slumping forward as she let out the breath she'd held. While she had the opportunity, she pulled out the leftover meat from the night before and sandwiched it between the heels of the loaf, which Eevid and Goziva refused to eat, before taking it with her to her room.

Cinza squeezed into the tiny space she called her own, the door unable to open all the way since her mattress took up most of the floor. Crammed between the wall and her bed, her desk was the only other piece of furniture in the room, and the drawers could only open a few inches. She resisted the urge to reach into the furthest drawer and dig out the bracelet hidden in the back.

The single piece of jewelry was the only thing she'd been able to keep from her mother. She rarely pulled it out for fear of her stepfamily finding it, but sometimes in the middle of the night when her loneliness and misery became too great, she'd take it out. The cold jewels were no substitute for her mother's love, yet she felt comforted when she slipped it around her wrist.

Glancing around her tiny room for evidence of tampering, Cinza swallowed her sadness. There were no decorations on her walls, and the bedding was the same as she'd had the past six years, since Eevid claimed the funds ran out before she found a suitable set for Cinza.

Sighing, she tucked her feet beside her on the mattress as she took another dry bite of bread and meat. She hadn't had time for breakfast since her stepmother had thrust the letter into her hands and demanded she take it to her father the second she'd dried them from washing the dishes after Eevid and Goziva's morning meal, so her stomach appreciated the food, as meager as it was.

She tried to pull her mind back to her daily tasks when a hard chest and golden irises stole into her thoughts.

Running into Armyn had been a shock. She hadn't expected to see him, even though the king had announced his safe return, and the hard alpha she'd crashed into barely resembled the cocky one who'd left shortly before her mother's death. Sure, he had the same blue feathers and shortened gold hair, but his aura screamed danger. Even the briefest glance showed an alpha capable of killing if the situation needed it.

A shudder ran through her, and Cinza told herself the racing of her heart was from the fear he inspired and nothing else.

When her womb clenched, she let out an audible gasp and almost dropped the last of her sandwich, scrambling to her knees to crawl across the narrow mattress to the bottle of pills resting on the desk. She usually took them as soon as she awoke, but raised voices at the end of the hall where her father and Eevid slept woke her this morning, and she'd slipped from her bed amid the argument to start breakfast, hoping to appease her stepmother's temper once her father left.

Tiny red pills tumbled into her palm. Carefully putting the extras back into the bottle, she raised two to her lips and swallowed them dry, taking the last bite of her food to force them down. Her stepmother may do nothing else for Cinza, but she'd provided the suppressants since the beginning of Cinza's first heat, and for that at least, Cinza was grateful. The thought of suffering through a cycle alone was terrifying, but thinking of easing it with anyone left her stomach rolling with distaste. There was only one alpha she'd ever considered allowing into her nest.

Shaking her head, Cinza forced herself to focus. The life she'd pictured before no longer seemed like an option. So much had changed, including herself, even if Armyn didn't see it.

"Cinza!"

The yell caused her to jump and scramble from her bed. Grabbing her basket of dirty things in case Eevid was in the hallway, she stepped out of her little closet as if she'd only been collecting laundry, but there was no one in sight. Slipping the basket back inside her room, she silently closed the door and moved toward the stairs before the yell came again, drawing her into Goziva's bedroom.

Her stepsister's room was at least four times bigger than hers. The fourposter bed alone wouldn't have fit inside Cinza's room, much less the dresser, armoire, vanity, and the two night tables.

Clasping her hands in front of her, Cinza bowed her head and waited for whatever it was Eevid would demand of her next. She was lacing up the back of Goziva's dress but turned to Cinza once she finished.

"We're leaving to go shopping and visit the seamstress. If she doesn't get started on our dresses right away, they won't be ready in time for the ball."

Surprise bloomed inside Cinza's chest and she dared to raise her gaze to Eevid's, thinking she could go too, until her stepmother burst that bubble of hope.

"You'll be fine with something from one of those musty chests in the shed, but it better be presentable. I won't have you making a fool of me or Goziva when you arrive with us."

"She can't arrive with us! I don't understand why the queen wants her there. No one else does. You should make her walk, Mama. She won't fit in the carriage with my dress anyway."

Goziva's voice grated on Cinza's nerves, but one unexpected part of her sentence caught Cinza's attention.

The queen wanted her at the ball.

Holding her breath, she pulled her attention back to Eevid.

"Her father wouldn't allow it. Anyway, I expect you to have something decent. And you can clean the shed while you're out there. There's no telling what critters are living amid those old trunks."

Swallowing, Cinza nodded and turned to leave, but froze in the doorway when Eevid's voice rose behind her.

"Be careful of the prongs on the locks, dear. We wouldn't want another accident."

Heart stuttering, Cinza's throat closed on a sob as she rushed from the room to the sound of Goziva's laughter.

Chapter 10

Armyn

Armyn fought the urge to glance at his mother as he rose from kissing the newcomer's knuckles. The woman had multicolored wings and sparkling blue eyes, giving her Fayrie heritage away. She beamed a smile at him, hiding the intuition and wisdom he'd sensed when she first stepped into the room.

"It's a pleasure to meet you, Mrs. Faeluna."

His words were a lie. He felt nothing but self-contempt and rage with every breath, but he'd exerted the worst of it on a dummy in the royal family's private gym. He couldn't forgive himself if he hurt yet another able-bodied warrior, so he'd destroyed the mock flesh. Whoever found it would probably fear a monster had snuck into the castle.

He released the woman's hand and slid his gaze to his parents, smoothing his features to hide the annoyance wriggling within his own private hell. His mother had hired the woman several months ago to help coordinate his homecoming ball, but when she'd told Armyn's father how efficient and smart Faeluna was, they'd both agreed to promote her. She was now the official Royal Public Relations and Affairs Manager.

Which meant he'd have her by his side until he proved he could mingle with the public without causing damage to the family's reputation. There were already rumors circulating about him.

"I'm glad to meet you, Prince Armyn."

The vibrant lady turned toward his parents, curtsying as was proper, before smiling toward Armyn's mother.

"You were right, Your Majesty. He *is* strikingly handsome. The flowers you chose will accentuate his blues and golds."

Armyn watched as his mother returned the Fayrie's smile, realizing the lady had won her way into his mother's heart.

Was there more here? Were they scheming as women, especially mothers, did? Should he be wary of spending time alone with this stranger?

His hackles rose even as he reminded himself that his pedigree meant he couldn't marry anyone who wasn't high class, which meant this beta woman was not eligible. He knew his next mission was to assimilate back into civilian life and find a mate, but the task seemed too large to even contemplate, much less figure out how to untangle by himself.

The petite lady swiveled to face him, pulling a device from her pocket before addressing him.

"There are things we need to discuss and more we need to accomplish before the ball tomorrow night. Walk with me, Your Highness."

A sliver of respect slid behind his breastbone. Most middle class couldn't traverse the social niceties with strength and poise, yet here this woman was, basically bossing him around with nary a pause. Her self-assuredness both concerned and relieved him.

She turned toward the door and waved for him to follow.

One last glance at his parents showed his father's nod of encouragement and his mother's expression of mirth. She enjoyed the woman's no-nonsense approach, which no doubt had flustered his father in the beginning as well. The king had his board of advisors, but this little beta stood in a realm of her own. She wouldn't confine herself to meeting rooms or set times.

Armyn unglued his talons from the marble and caught up with the woman, her shorter strides carrying her farther than he thought possible in such a short time.

The next few hours would be a test of his sanity. She rattled off his schedule, highlighting how little time he'd have to himself between now and the ball.

Swallowing his sigh, he strode beside her as they headed straight for the seamstress. First stop, a new dress coat to match the flowers his mother had chosen.

***

Torture.

He'd found a hell almost as bad as the days he'd spent captured.

His fear during those horrible hours had been all-consuming, much like the anger currently festering within his chest. He had no way of releasing the infection, the crowd of people watching his every move.

Armyn didn't bother to don a smile, merely kissed another gloved hand and kept his face as neutral as possible. The urge to roar and spread his wings to push the women away from him was great, but he held them tucked against his back, their weight another source of guilt.

He'd survived. So had Quasim, but not whole, and his friend still wasn't there to welcome him.

It wasn't fair.

Armyn cut the thoughts off, shoving them deep into the seething horror bubbling in his chest. He pulled his mind back to the present, not paying attention to Faeluna as she talked about the most recent woman presented to him. He trained his gaze above the omega's head, keeping up with the niceties with as little involvement as he could.

When the woman curtsied and moved away, Armyn flicked his gaze to his personal tormentor.

Her shrewd perusal made him stiffen. In the scant few hours they'd interacted, he'd learned she didn't need words to communicate. She read him like a book, mentioning counseling more than once as she dragged him around the castle. Without shifting or giving any physical indication of her thoughts, she excused the next woman with the promise of a formal introduction soon.

He'd thought he would have his emotions under control by now, but without solitude, he lacked a way to expel the excess.

"Prince Armyn?"

"Yes, Mrs. Faeluna."

"May I suggest a beverage? Something to help you relax? What would you like?"

He almost refused on principle, but the tightness beside her eyes made him agree to a drink. When he ordered one alcoholic and one non-alcoholic beverage, her shoulders relaxed.

"There are still dozens upon dozens of high-class ladies to greet. We can't dally for too long, so you have five minutes."

He didn't take even two, slamming both drinks and earning a glare from his Fayrie slave driver. She asked if he was ready to resume, to which he nodded his agreement.

"Prince Armyn, meet Madam Eevid and her daughter, Lady Goziva."

A pompously dressed woman and her equally garnished daughter curtsied, their black hair and heavily painted faces twisting his guts. Nothing about them seemed genuine. Something in their mannerisms kick-started the same wriggling dread he'd felt before his team's last mission. He wouldn't ignore it again, even if he had no obvious course of action in this formal situation.

"We're honored to meet you, Prince Armyn."

The older woman's voice caused his premonition to grow, her sickly sweet tone and fluttering eyelashes much the same as the other ladies he'd "met" tonight, but she oozed a warped aura. Her daughter sized him up, thinking he focused solely on her mother, but he noted the same greedy expression before she smoothed her features.

The younger lady's stance morphed into a faux innocence, her eyes widening before dropping in an exaggerated display of shyness. She stayed looking at his feet as though he would coax her attention to his, but he didn't offer to kiss her hand.

Madam Eevid stepped forward and extended her fingers, leaving him no choice but to bend over her knuckles. Unable to force himself to lay his lips against her glove, he hovered an inch above her clad digits before he rose and glanced at Faeluna.

She interpreted his look and began further introductions as he gave a similar mock kiss to Lady Goziva's glove.

"Madam Eevid married Administrator Glashu about five years ago, after his late wife passed away."

Armyn held his wings tight to his body; the shock of hearing Cinza's last name in the same sentence as this gaudy woman's making him fight the urge to strike out with his most potent weapons. He'd ruined more men's lives than he cared to admit with his wings, yet never had he struck a female. The sudden desire to maim a member of the weaker gender had never existed before, yet his instincts cried out for him to attack this enemy.

Except the woman and her daughter couldn't be his enemy. He knew nothing about them, other than they obviously wanted the prestige of his favor.

"It was a horrible tragedy. My heart broke for my sweet alpha as he mourned the loss of such a kind woman. We found sharing the grief made it more bearable."

His eyes swung to the overdressed beta, his hatred for her growing with every syllable she spoke. Each word was a lie. His intuition had never failed him, so he had no reason to ignore it.

When the younger lady slid uncomfortably close and batted her lashes before she spoke, Armyn's disgust grew to an all-time high.

"Administrator Glashu is such a noble alpha. He's done so much for your family and the kingdom. He considers me his own child. It's amazing to have a powerful father figure."

She leaned closer and batted her lashes yet again before stage-whispering to him.

"I would love to have such a noble and strong alpha as my mate. I hope you'll save a dance for me later."

Armyn nearly choked on her perfume, the cloying scent attacking his senses before he recognized her ploy. She meant to hide her natural beta dynamic by drowning herself in an artificial omega pheromone. Although he could mate whomever he chose, Armyn desired a full bond, which wasn't possible with a beta. It was a struggle, but he didn't cut the woman down with his words or slash her open with the talons on his wing tips. Instead, he cocked an eyebrow and forced himself to leave all other reactions absent.

A quick flick of his gaze toward Faeluna prompted the end of the "greeting", but as they turned to leave, so did he.

Broiling fury and disgust shifted from the ones in front of him to the one who wasn't.

Armyn had bumped into Cinza the day before. She hadn't warned him about her new family. She could have at least hinted at the change, but she'd left him to meet them in the most public and ridiculous way, without bothering to present herself at the same time.

His sense of betrayal may not make sense, but he couldn't see past the emotion. First she'd struck him deep where he had no defenses—mentioning his best friend's absence—then she'd withheld important life changes from him.

His anger grew as another worry slid between his ribs.

Had it been easy for her to not mention her father's new wife because she'd found a mate of her own and no longer lived in her father's household? Was she not presented with her stepsister because she had a new title? He cursed himself for not checking her scent during their hallway interlude.

Had she made good on the words she'd taunted him with during their last encounter before he left? Had another alpha had claimed her?

Without meaning to, every mangled emotion within his chest focused on the one who probably deserved it least, but he had no other target to aim them toward.

So, with teeth grinding and blood pumping in his ears, he sought the omega he'd dreamed of for years. The one who'd taken his anger as a child and morphed it into something more complex.

He'd do whatever it took to get the truth out of her and drain himself of the need to understand. He'd rid himself of whatever infatuation he'd carried for her.

He'd crush Cinza and free himself from the ugly emotions warping his insides.

Chapter 11

Cinza

The floral scents floating in the air were almost enough to let her forget the stifling party at her back. The gardens were her second favorite place in the palace, and she'd often visited them when she'd attended classes in the grand halls, but it'd been so long since she'd been out here, she'd forgotten how soothing the tinkling fountains could be.

Sucking in another deep breath to ease the turmoil in her chest, a familiar, heady, masculine scent snuck in to ruin her attempts at finding peace.

Armyn.

Instinct urging her to run, Cinza spun to dart toward the stairs off the balcony, only to crash into a hard wall of muscle. Massive wings flared in agitation as large hands shot out to grip her arms. He righted her with a jerk before yanking his hands away as if she'd burned him.

She tipped her head back to meet his golden irises. Fear speared through her at the anger filling his eyes.

"Why didn't you tell me?"

The words ground together as if he barely held back a growl, and for a moment Cinza's mind blanked.

Tell him her world crumbled when he left?

Tell him she felt like a shell of her former self?

Tell him how desperately she'd missed him in the beginning, needing to tell someone how horrible she felt for causing her mother's death and how much she hated Eevid and Goziva?

His scowl deepened when she didn't answer. He stepped forward and towered over her. Cinza shuffled backward until the railing blocked her escape. He crowded her against it, leaving only a breath between their chests.

"W-What do you mean?"

"About your mother. About that horrible thing your father apparently married when his bonded died. It's a disgrace."

The anger she saw coiling through Armyn seemed disproportionate to the issue at hand. Yes, it was unusual for an alpha to take a second wife if he survived the death of the first, but it wasn't unheard of. And he'd clearly met her stepmother and sister. She couldn't fault him for his opinion there.

Eyes trying to dart around his massive frame, a shiver ran down her spine at the thought that they'd followed him and would find them together on the balcony. It wasn't her reputation she worried about. No, it was the threat Eevid had made as Cinza helped them dress.

"If I so much as see you glance in the prince's direction, I'll tell him every sordid detail of your mother's painful death. How your immaturity and carelessness crushed her spine and impaled her on the prongs of a lock only opened because of you."

Cinza's stomach lurched, bile burning the back of her throat.

"I-I need to go."

She tried to sidestep down the railing, but Armyn mirrored her movement and shot his hands out to grip the banister on either side of her hips, forcing Cinza to freeze.

"You're not going anywhere until you tell me what happened."

His growl stole her will and scrambled her mind, the deep reverberations awakening organs she'd never used before. He leaned closer, giving her no choice but to bow backward. Her hands clenched on the smooth metal were the only thing preventing her from falling into the flowers below. Too much further and she wouldn't be able to keep her balance.

Her mouth spoke despite the rushing in her ears.

"There was an accident. She died. Father married Eevid to look after me while he was gone on business trips."

She tried not to think of the events as she said them, but tears still pricked the back of her eyes. Her heart pounded within her ribcage, memories constricting her lungs and making her head spin.

"Please. I need to go. I-I can't be here with you."

Armyn's growl deepened, sending a shudder through her body. His hand left the banister beside her, and for a moment she thought he would let her escape.

Fingers tangled in the hair at the base of her skull, ending the illusion of freedom. Armyn crushed her to his chest and forced her head further back.

He ran his nose along the column of her neck and across her bare shoulder before he switched to the other side. Her nipples turned traitorous, tightening to diamond points beneath the cerulean fabric of her dress.

The one her mother had died finding.

She didn't know what happened to the trunk that killed her mother, but Cinza had found the blue dress she'd been holding crammed into the top of another. Someone had gone through the chests, carelessly tossing things about and not sealing them properly, and it ended up being the only dress not spoiled by the dampness in the shed or the moths that had made the fabrics their home. For a moment she'd considered the gown cursed, but she remembered her mother's joy upon finding it and knew her mother would have wanted her to wear it.

And a small part of her had wanted Armyn to see her in it.

The flick of something hot and wet against the lobe of her ear jerked her back to her present situation. She couldn't help the way her body responded to the growling alpha pinning her in his arms, dragging in deep breaths of her scent.

"What else haven't you told me, Cinza? What else has changed?"

A whine escaped her throat before she could stop it. The threat threaded within his words sent a shiver through her body. Her hands still clung to the rails behind her, but Armyn's hold had almost lifted her from her feet, only the toes of her shoes now scraping the tiles.

"N-nothing. Everything. I don't know what you want."

Scalding liquid spilled from her eyes, burning tracks down her cheeks. Her entire body trembled, and her breath shuddered as she sucked in what little air his arms allowed.

"Has another alpha marked you, Cinza? Have you been claimed?"

His voice had dropped to a whisper as his lips brushed against the skin of her neck. Shameful dampness built between her trembling thighs as his words brought back images from her dreams. Images of things she'd never experienced at the hands of a real man.

"No."

The word was nothing more than an exhale escaping without thought. It would have been smarter to tell him she was. To avoid more confusion between them and give her an excuse to put distance between them.

But she couldn't lie. Not to Armyn. Not about that.

Armyn jerked away as voices approached. Cinza's feet landed on the balcony as his grip left her hair. She watched his mouthwatering chest heaving in the twinkling lights strung above, but the feral look left his eyes.

More sound intruded as their surroundings bled back into focus, the rising notes of a violin drifting out to where they stood an arm's length apart, trying to understand what had just happened.

"Dance with me."

Her brows furrowed at the hand extended in her direction. It hadn't been a request, and she knew Armyn would get what he wanted, no matter what her opinion may be.

Eyes darting around at the other people who'd stepped out onto the balcony, she realized there were other pairs dancing, and for a moment she let go of the fear. Placing her fingers in his palm, she let him pull her closer and wrap his other hand around her waist. There was more space between them than there had been mere seconds earlier, and for some undecipherable reason, it felt wrong.

Lifting her gaze to Armyn's, she stared up into his eyes as their bodies swayed. She could see the pain, the confusion, and the apology she knew would never pass his lips.

And she forgave him. Despite everything she'd been through, everything he'd put her through, the feelings that had bloomed in their youth were still there. She still loved him, and she could finally accept that was what it was.

The anger Armyn had shown, the fear… she could see they came from the same feeling churning within her. He just hadn't accepted it yet.

Cinza hoped he never did, because they couldn't be together with her stepmother's threat hanging over her. It might seem as simple as explaining what happened, but she knew she couldn't look in his eyes and tell him she'd killed her mother. He could crush her with a single disgusted glare.

He couldn't know.

The song ended, and they slowed to a standstill. A flash of gaudy color to her right caught her attention, and Cinza's eyes locked on the angry face of her stepsister.

Goziva flashed a mean smile from the doorway before turning and stomping inside, no doubt going to fetch her mother and tell her what she'd seen. Heart leaping into her throat, Cinza's head shook as she looked back at Armyn.

"I must go. I can't be here. I..."

She swallowed and steeled herself for what she had to say. Armyn's brows had lowered again, the tension that had left his body as they danced returning to his shoulders.

"I can't be with you."

Her vision swam as she forced out the words, the last of her heart crumbling into the void in her chest. Pain pulsed with each stuttering breath, and she took a step back as she shook her head again.

Chapter 12

Armyn

She'd given him peace only to snatch it away with a few words.

Unable to decipher the conglomeration of emotions blaring from her eyes, his body refused to move while the hurt of her declaration sank deep into his bones. The fury she'd banked with her delicious scent came roaring back, and his feet moved before he gave them permission.

She reached the bottom of the stairs before he caught up with her, the gleaming locks of her hair teasing him as they trailed behind her in the breeze. Despite his anger, he couldn't forget the tears she'd shed, so he resisted the urge to yank her backward by the silvery strands and instead wrapped his hand around her upper arm.

Cinza's slight weight made her no match for him, his grip stopping her forward momentum so suddenly her body jerked as though it'd hit a wall.

"Let me go."

Her voice sounded thick with tears, adding confusion to his anger.

"I've told you before. Never."

"You must."

"No, I won't."

Shimmering blue irises reflected the moonlight back up to him as she swiveled her head to meet his furious gaze.

Her tears only fueled his rage.

"Hot one moment. Cold the next. This is payback, isn't it?"

"No, Ar—"

"Don't you fucking dare say my name. You just came alive in my arms, melting against me and flowering the air with your delicious scent. Your sweet lips tempt me at every turn, and your tight little body begs for my knot. You're unclaimed and ripe for the picking. Don't you dare try to run away now."

How she understood his deep, rumbled words he didn't know, but the fight drained out of her muscles and heat crept up her cheeks. He wanted to crush her to him and find the calm she'd graced him with scant moments ago, but when he released her arm to caress her face, she stiffened.

"Stop. I need you to leave me alone."

Cinza darted forward on a sob, but Armyn had years of training and much quicker reflexes than she did. He lunged forward and snagged her wrist.

She wrenched downward, trying to unbalance him with the training she'd had as a teen, but he tightened his grip and stood as unmovable as a mountain. A small pop reached his ears before tiny jewels scattered over the paving stones with little tinkling skips.

Cinza's quiet cry broke through his resolve, but when she fought harder, he yanked her toward him. Intending to wrap her in his arms, her tiny fist caught him off guard. It hit directly below his diaphragm, making his chest seize as the organ tightened in agony. His grip slipped, but he twisted his hips and caught purchase at the top of her glove. It slipped down her arm as Cinza spun around and batted her wings in his face before her foot lifted to carry her forward. Her sobs attacked him worse than her fist had, but he sucked in a breath.

Releasing it on a growl, he reached beyond the fragile wings and wove his fingers in the hair along her scalp, but her hands shot upward to grab his arm.

One gloved hand landed on the right side of his wrist—the sliver of skin exposed as his shirt sleeve rode up from their scuffle, noting the smooth glide of warm fabric. When her bare fingers wrapped around the other side of his wrist, he froze.

Rough callouses rubbed against the sensitive inner flesh of his forearm, her glove dangling from his fingertips as his gaze narrowed to her tiny knuckles.

Thin white stripes gleamed in the moonlight, the raised scars uneven and jagged. His omega shouldn't carry such signs of abuse, not if he hadn't been the cause.

And he'd never hurt her like this.

The signs of hard labor shone on her skin, etched into her delicate digits and obvious in the swollen joints.

She froze as he snarled.

Cinza's misery arrowed straight to his soul, cracking it open and making him want to sob even as a tempestuous rage threatened to blank his vision.

When he whispered her name, she broke.

"Please, Armyn. For my sake, let me go," she managed between sobs.

His grip loosened as he warred within himself. He wanted to gather her close and carry her away from whatever hurt her. Until he realized *he* was the source of her misery. Indecisive, he watched as her wings shimmered like glass in the soft light of the moon, her sobs shaking her entire body.

When a commotion began on the terrace, she stifled her crying.

Through gritted teeth, her sob sliced through his chest as her leg shot backward.

Blinding pain raced up from his shin as her heel slammed against his leg. She slipped from his hold as he grunted in agony, escaping the gardens before he could catch her again.

Armyn stared in numb confusion as her beautiful blue dress disappeared into the night. Her glove dangled from his hand until the noise from behind him broke his stupor. Armyn balled up the material before cramming it in his suit pocket. When he turned to resume his duties, holding on to the off-center silence in his mind, something sparkled on the smooth paver under his talons.

Crouching down, Armyn gathered the scattered jewels, staring at the tiny things nestled in his palm until recognition settled over him.

He knew the sparkling bracelet they used to create. Cinza's mother had always worn it, no matter the season or occasion.

Guilt resurfaced.

He'd broken her mother's favorite piece of jewelry in his need to possess her.

A woman's silhouette shone from the top of the stairs, breaking his concentration. Stuffing the ruined memento into his pocket, he climbed the steps one at a time, his thoughts gaining speed as he ascended toward the party.

He had many questions, none of which Cinza seemed prepared to answer, so he'd find them elsewhere.

He would not let his omega escape for long.

Chapter 13

Cinza

She didn't dare risk going inside to find their driver, so Cinza ran.

Down the long drive, through the gates, into the town outside the palace grounds. She didn't even stop for the startled guards who called after her as her wings propelled her faster than her feet alone could run.

Tears filled her vision, making everything a blur. Light flashed by between bouts of darkness, and she stumbled along as her energy ran out and her feet slowed. She got turned around on the wrong block but eventually found her way home.

Knowing her stepmother locked the front door when she left, Cinza slipped around to the back. The gate creaked as she walked through into the backyard, but there was no one in the house to be alerted by her movements. Her father would be stuck at the ball until it ended in the early hours of the morning, and she doubted anything would pry Eevid and Goziva away from their chance to advance before then either.

Which was why she froze in shock when her stepmother moved into the light above the backdoor.

"I warned you, Cinza, but you just couldn't listen."

Cinza took a step back as Eevid came forward, instincts screaming she was in danger.

"All you had to do was stay away from the prince and your little secret would have stayed with us. Now Goziva is telling him all about it while I had to come back here to deal with you."

Cinza's tears dried as she tried to figure out what Eevid had planned. She was still panting for breath, her sides aching from the long run as she sobbed, and she wasn't sure if she'd be able to exert herself further.

"I should have dealt with you the same way I did your mother, but it was nice having a free maid. Did you know suppressants can be toxic if you take too much at once? I'd planned to stage an overdose since you were clearly so grief-stricken over your mother's death, but your father's return delayed it, and then you made yourself useful."

Eevid continued moving closer as she spoke, but her words had rooted Cinza in place. Confusion jumbled her thoughts, but dawning horror spread through her as the meaning of the words became clear.

"You..."

She couldn't force out the words. Her mouth hung open, her tongue unwilling to give life to the truth.

"Of course it was me. Did you really think you swung that gown with enough force to knock the lid closed? Those things were damned heavy, and she had me opening one after another just to find *that*."

The scorn was clear in her tone, but Cinza was more shocked by the aplomb with which Eevid admitted to murder.

"And now you've made yourself more trouble than you're worth, but there are better things to do with you than kill you."

Cinza was still struggling with her new knowledge when Eevid grabbed her arm. Pulled along the path away from the house, Cinza didn't think to struggle until the shed came into view.

"There are plenty of alphas eager to take an omega no matter her willingness, and they'll pay good money for it, too. Your father's getting stingy with the credits, but Goziva and I can continue to live in comfort for a while with what I'll make off of you. He'll think you finally broke and ran away, and Prince Armyn can comfort Goziva through the tough loss of her poor stepsister."

Cinza tried to dig her heels in as Eevid chuckled, but the woman was larger than her and hadn't exhausted herself from running. Turning to twist Cinza's arm up to mash her wrist against her spine, Eevid gripped Cinza's shoulder with her free hand and marched them forward.

The shed loomed in front of them. It was in the far corner of their property, far enough from the main house and the neighbors that no light reached it.

The wood of one door scratched her cheek as Eevid smashed her into it to pull the other open. Growing desperate, Cinza thrashed, trying to beat the woman behind her with her wings, but Eevid was stronger than she looked. Pulling Cinza's arm higher until she cried out in pain, Eevid maintained control, pushing Cinza into the open doorway before a heel to her bottom sent Cinza sprawling onto the floor.

"You'll remain here until I have your purchase settled. After that, you'll no longer be my concern. I hope you enjoyed your dance with the prince, since it's the last time a male is going to be that respectful when he touches you."

Tossing the cascade of blonde hair out of her face, Cinza looked back just in time to see the door swing shut, the click of the lock resounding through the shed. She leaped to her feet, but with no light to illuminate the floor, she was cautious as she made her way back to the door. No matter how hard she turned the knobs and pushed on the wooden panels, they refused to budge. Even when she took a few steps back and rammed the doors with her shoulder, she did nothing more than hurt herself.

Collapsing to the floor on a sob as she cradled her throbbing arm, her mind replayed Eevid's words. She couldn't let that evil woman win and go on fooling her father. She wouldn't allow herself to be sold like livestock.

But she couldn't plan an escape in the dark when she couldn't see what she had to work with.

Shuffling her way to the wall, she leaned against it and pulled her knees to her chest. It was warm enough in the shed she didn't have to worry about getting chilled during the night, and come morning, she should have enough light to look for a way out.

***

By the time the sun was directly overhead, Cinza had gone through every chest. More than once. There was nothing there.

Drenched in sweat, the only tools in the shed were simple gardening supplies. The tiny, palm-sized shovel had too much of a curve to fit in the narrow slit between the doors.

Letting herself slide down the wall, she panted for breath as she thought through her options. The comfortably warm shed had grown stifling, the heat of the sun shining through the tiny windows near the roof having no way to escape.

Much like Cinza.

Shoving that thought away, she turned the shovel in her hands. While small, it was a sturdy piece of equipment, and despite her attempts to flatten the metal, it refused to change shape. The tines of the handheld rake were too thick to wedge between the doors, and there was nothing else she could find to help her.

Another thing missing was water.

The old sink in the back of the shed had seemed to offer relief when the morning sun gilded it, but it turned into broken hope as the knobs twisted and released nothing more than a spray of dust. Even after checking the hoses beneath, Cinza couldn't get it to give her the fluid she desperately needed.

As the light from the sun moved across the wall, she gave up hope for food. The gnawing in her belly was easy to ignore, but her parched throat burned more with each breath. The beautiful gown was a sorry sight, wrinkled from her night spent on the hard floor and drenched in sweat to the point it clung to her.

Sighing, Cinza tried not to let the fear pull her under. She forced herself to stand, deciding on her next plan.

The windows were tiny and almost twice her height from the floor. She couldn't fly through midair for long distances the way the Raptyrs could, her Fayrie wings more delicate, but she could lift herself to the window for a short time. She hoped they were larger than they appeared from the floor.

Standing back and looking up toward her source of light, she put her hands on her hips and huffed.

"Why the hell is this building so tall?"

Her voice echoed back at her. Shaking her head, she let her hands drop and gave her wings a few experimental flicks before launching herself toward the window facing away from the house.

Wings fluttering, she could feel her energy waning even as she rose from the floor. She was already struggling when her fingertips scrabbled against the glass, wings unused to the strain of lifting her weight.

The window was no bigger than she'd thought. Perhaps wide enough for her to wiggle her shoulders through, but her wings would never fit. Opening the glass to let out some of the heat, she dropped back to the floor, landing harder than intended. It took everything in her to hold back the tears of frustration, but if she let them come, she knew it would be twice as hard to stop.

And she couldn't afford the loss of fluid.

Dry tongue slipping out to lick dryer lips, her eyes moved back to the broken sink. She'd never gone so long without water, and already her body felt like it was shriveling from the lack. With the sun dropping in the sky, she wouldn't have light for much longer, and she decided she should try to fix the sink instead of trying to get the other windows open.

She started at the top, turning and checking everything she could from the handles to the spout. The hand rake might have been useless for trying to pry open the door, but it worked as a wrench.

Forcing two tines around the ends of the hoses, she loosened them enough to pull them off the faucet once she moved under the sink. Dried gunk fell out, showing how long the sink had sat unused. With a grimace, she continued, removing the other ends. One hose was so full of grime it was stiff, but the other didn't seem as bad. Pushing a prong into the opening in the pipe the hose had attached to, Cinza scraped but came out with nothing more than a smear of slime. On the verge of giving up as the last of her light waned, she reached out to twist the knob on the pipe behind it once again, hoping she'd accidentally turned it off.

She swallowed hard when nothing happened, but as she turned to crawl from the tight space beneath the sink, a sparkle caught her eye.

One slow drop grew. Wavered. Dripped.

Tears burst from her as her hand shot out to catch the next. She licked it from her palm before reaching for another. Her sobs turned into laughter as the drops came faster. The light gave way to darkness before it increased to a steady drip, but it was more than she'd had before, and she was grateful.

There was no telling how long she lay next to the sink, one hand cupped under the dripping pipe before sucking away the moisture, but eventually her thirst eased enough to let her slip into sleep. Her belly was still tight with hunger, but at least she wouldn't die of dehydration. Even if she didn't find a way out of the shed before Eevid returned, there'd be an opportunity to escape at some point, and now she wouldn't be too weak to take it.

Chapter 14

Armyn

His eyes felt gritty and dry, his lids uncomfortable as they scraped up and down his lenses.

It'd been three days since his homecoming ball. He hadn't slept but a handful of hours since then, and not a single sleep session had lasted longer than thirty minutes.

To add more chaos to the jumbled mass of nonsense banging around inside his head, Armyn had opened a letter from Blaide the morning after the party and learned that his youngest team member was in the city, bunkered down in a safe place to enjoy his newly found omega mate. Blaide had mentioned Ursuli's whereabouts and living conditions, adding on a few light jokes to emphasize how *not okay* their medic was.

Armyn's duties had kept him busy the rest of the day, but yesterday he'd taken a trip, hoping for advice from his eldest teammate if Blaide's warning rang false.

Ursuli had been fully ensconced in his own new mate, so Armyn left without asking. His brother didn't deserve to have Armyn's problems mar his newly bonded life. He was truly happy for Ursuli and Blaide, even though jealousy plagued him.

So he'd returned home just as confused as he had been when Cinza ran from him.

Last night had been difficult, his dread startling him from his fitful dozing over and over until he'd thrust his private balcony doors open. His urge to dive off the balcony and take a midnight soar over the city died as he studied the lights glowing from the cityscape.

He couldn't risk flying straight to Cinza's house and seeing her look at him with such pain in her eyes again.

Despite many attempts to speak to Cinza's father alone the night of the ball, he hadn't had the opportunity. The man was well-known and deeply respected, keeping him in demand, but watching him from across the room only increased Armyn's dread.

Administrator Glashu looked fine on the surface with his hair and clothes well kept, but Armyn saw how his stress showed in the lines of his forehead and how dull his eyes were. He didn't smile nearly as much as he used to, the laugh lines he previously sported less pronounced because of his lack of mirth.

Armyn only saw him with his new wife when he spoke to the inner circle of high-class royalty, the woman clinging to his arm and simpering her way into every conversation.

After Cinza's disappearance, her stepsister interjected herself into his path at every opportunity until Armyn nearly lashed out. He kept himself under control simply because the beta woman's advances were so blatant, he could almost have pitied her if she weren't so persistent. At the end of the night, he'd been relieved Cinza's family had left, even though he hadn't had time to speak with her father.

Armyn had learned patience during his time with his teammates, but with his little Fayrie involved, he found it much more difficult to wait.

Which was why he'd barged into his father's meeting without an invitation.

The round table provided more than enough room for the king and his advisors, so when Armyn arrived, they'd pulled up another ornate chair and sat him next to his father.

If Armyn couldn't speak with Cinza's father despite being in the same castle with him, then he'd make sure his duties put him in the same room as the advisor.

The topics ranged far and wide, but the king addressed each problem with succinct plans of action, and Armyn appreciated for the first time how epically stressful this kind of responsibility could be. He'd learned a different strength in the military, so seeing the mental pressure required for ruling caught him unawares. He'd expected it to be like leading his unit, but the kingdom was so much larger, with much different concerns than a group of men just trying to stay alive another day.

How was his father still so youthful?

Leaning his elbow on his armrest, Armyn surveyed the king's advisors, noting their age and areas of expertise. Their jobs were no doubt just as stressful as the king's were, but each one seemed more than competent to complete their tasks. None were as young as Armyn, but three of the eight had already chosen their replacements. The understudies listened with rapt attention, even when it wasn't their turn to present whatever problems they brought to the throne, which showed how right they were to receive the burdens of responsibility.

Turning to inspect his father for the first time since their reunion, Armyn's relief at seeing his predecessor still vibrant and stern eased the worry behind his breastbone. Even though the king would pass the crown to him during his coronation ceremony, Armyn was glad he'd have his father's guidance for many years to come. He'd have to prove himself before the advisors took him seriously.

When the meeting adjourned, Armyn stood in unison with everyone else and thanked his father for allowing him to stay.

"I expect you to be in here more often, son."

"Of course, Father. There's still much for me to learn."

Nodding before he turned to one of his advisors, the king dismissed Armyn. The second he was free, Armyn searched the room for Cinza's father and almost snarled when he spotted the male's wings turning into the hall. Skirting around the fringes of the room, he avoided anyone approaching him, too focused on his task to worry about being rude.

Armyn stepped into the hallway and followed the sounds of Luzor Glashu's talons clicking on the marble floor. He called out before the alpha closed his office door behind him, causing the older male to pause.

"Ah, Prince Armyn. May I help you?"

"Not with anything official. I wanted to offer my condolences about your late wife and ask you a few questions."

"Of course, my prince. Would you like to sit in my office?"

After agreeing to the offer, Armyn passed by the other alpha and fought not to scrunch his nose. The male's scent, while still light and healthy, carried a bitter twang of loneliness and the sour stench of depression.

Declining to accept the better chair behind the other man's desk, he took his place in the plush seat on the other side. Cinza's father scowled a second before sitting in his normal spot.

"I truly am sorry for your loss. Your first mate was always a joy to be around, and I'm sure she is greatly missed."

"Thank you, Prince Armyn."

Armyn sucked in a breath and propped his elbows on his knees, meeting the alpha's gaze directly while trying to ease him out of being so formal.

"I must tell you the truth. I've been… fond of Cinza for some time."

At the man's blank look, Armyn steadied his nerves and thought of how perfectly she'd fit in his arms the other night. He nearly drowned in the memory of her budding pheromones. His soul yearned for hers even as he mourned over the trail of tears wetting her cheeks.

"More than fond. I want your permission to court your daughter, if she'll have me."

As understanding dawned on Luzor's features, the feathers on his forehead creased as memories of the past resurfaced. It was obvious he still missed his first wife.

Armyn's words slipped out without his permission.

"I… I don't want to hurt her, but I fear I already have. I need to make it right."

The abject misery and adrenaline-inducing fear shining from Cinza's orbs the night of the ball flashed through his vision.

Luzor's gaze sharpened, and he sat straighter at his prince's words, a flash of anger coming and going so quickly Armyn almost missed it.

"What do you mean?"

Resisting the urge to jab his fingers into his hair and yank, Armyn mimicked the other male's stance and stopped the twitching in his wings.

"I'm not sure. I need to know more about what happened while I was gone. Does she still live with you?"

"Of course she does. Why wouldn't she?"

"Most omegas her age have found their mate. They manage their own household and are raising their own hatchlings."

The older male's eyes glossed over, his mind searching for something Armyn couldn't help him with.

"Has she begun her cycles yet?"

The question snapped the alpha's attention to the present. He pierced his prince's eyes with a miserable look of his own.

"Well, I-I'm sure she has. At her age..."

"What do you mean?"

Luzor slumped against the back of his seat and rubbed his forehead with his fingers, defeat etched in his every feature.

"I've been traveling. Running away, really. Doing everything I can to escape my memories of Janine. I've never seen signs of Cinza having gone through a heat, but I'm gone often, and I doubt she'd come to me to discuss feminine issues."

Armyn swallowed the lump of chaos threatening to clog his throat. He wanted to shake the man and make him see reason. He wanted to slap some sense into him, knowing what he was about to say even though he hadn't spoken the words yet.

"I married Eevid because Cinza needed a woman's help. I thought I was doing the right thing, since I... Cinza looks so much like her mother, it hurts to be near her."

"So you abandoned her to the cold, heartless woman I met last night? I spoke to her for less than five minutes and I already know she isn't fit to be within a mile of Cinza's sweetness!"

He barely held back his roar, the snarled words vibrating from his chest and rattling the pens on the desk. Luzor straightened, face turning stern at Armyn's criticism.

"Eevid has been a good caretaker."

"Are you sure about that? Did you see your new wife at the ball last night?"

Luzor dropped his hand to his armrest and met Armyn's stare with a furrowed brow.

"Did you ever see her with Cinza? Did she introduce your daughter alongside her own when she was thrusting the girl at every eligible male in attendance? Did she even mention your daughter's name?"

The crease deepened in the other male's face.

"I spoke with my father last night. He hadn't realized you've been burying yourself in your work, volunteering for negotiations that require weeks of travel just to avoid your grief. Tell me, when's the last time you spent more than a week at home? When was the last time you actually looked at your daughter to see if she's made it past her grief, or if she needs the help of someone who cares?"

Sadness welled in the alpha's eyes, but Armyn's heart had gone cold. His duty had forced him away from his tiny Fayrie, but he'd thought she'd have a solid support system while he was gone. If he'd have known her father was abandoning her as well, he'd have shirked his responsibilities and stayed, crown be damned.

Except no one could have predicted her mother's death.

His instincts snapped to life, the dread simmering in his chest bursting through his frontal lobe as a horrible suspicion washed over him.

The night of the ball, when Cinza had first tried to run from him after their dance, her wing had reflected the light from the ballroom door back at him.

The memory grew and sharpened until he recognized who she'd seen over his shoulder.

"She fears Goziva."

"What? No. They have sisterly squabbles, but there's no reason for her to fear the girl."

"Yes, Luzor. She freaked out the night of the ball when she saw her stepsister. I suspect there's more to the issue."

"Wait, you saw Cinza during your homecoming ball? When?"

"Right before she ran from me in the gardens."

"She greeted you late in the festivities? Before the carriages lined up to leave?"

"No, she left long before then. It wasn't even midnight yet. I hadn't finished greeting arrivals when I stepped out for a moment and found her on the balcony."

The elder male's mouth turned down in a scowl.

"Eevid told me Cinza didn't leave until almost one-thirty in the morning, and that's why I didn't see her at breakfast."

Heart pounding in his head, Armyn stood.

"I do not trust your new wife, Administrator Glashu. Have you seen Cinza at all since the party?"

Luzor swallowed, his mind replaying the events since then. When he shook his head, Armyn gritted his teeth.

"How have you not noticed your daughter missing for three days?!"

"Our weekly dinner is tomorrow. She doesn't wake until after I leave for work, and I get home so late in the evenings she's already in bed when I return."

Gritting his teeth and forcing his muscles to act like statues of stone so he didn't lash out at the male, Armyn's mouth ran away from him as a new thought struck. One that explained too much to be wrong.

"Did you agree to give Cinza heat suppressants?"

Cinza's father burst into tears, whatever facade he'd hidden behind for years crumbling in the face of his sins.

"How could I have been so blind? An omega can't hide her heats from an alpha. Her scent has *never* changed. I just thought the grief... I thought she couldn't... I'm such a fucking fool."

Despite the agony leaking from his eyes and the misery pouring out in his every word, Luzor opened the top drawer of his desk and pulled something out. He stood and thrust a set of keys toward Armyn.

"Go. Here are my house keys. They'll open any door on my property. Find her. My wings aren't as fast as they once were."

Armyn took the keys and shoved them into his vest pocket, turning to the door without looking at the man's tortured face as he called instructions over his shoulder.

"Bring a few guards with you when you follow. Alert the royal infirmary of her imminent arrival. If she's been on heat suppressants since her mother's death..."

Armyn couldn't finish the thought, clamping his teeth together over the heated words threatening to spill from his mouth.

Cinza had needed him, but he'd been too blind to see it. He'd pushed her away.

Never again. He'd save her from her stepfamily and get her whatever help she required.

Because he admitted he needed her in his life. In his arms. In his bed. She already filled his every thought and owned whatever was left of his heart.

He'd once told her he was the only one allowed to torment her, but he'd left her defenseless. She'd been alone, facing whatever torture that vile woman had put her through, and he'd only heaped more abuse on her when he returned.

Never again.

Chapter 15

Cinza

Another day had come and gone. Cinza still couldn't escape the shed. Her little trickle of water kept the worst of the need for hydration at bay, but it was never enough to quench the thirst that seemed to grow worse with each passing hour.

She had tried to fly to another window to pry it open but hadn't been able to get more than a few inches from the ground before she collapsed. Hair plastered to her head with sweat, she'd resigned herself to waiting by her pipe and drinking as much as she could.

The cramps began the third night of her imprisonment. She didn't know if it was the lack of food or perhaps a contaminant in the water, but her belly roiled through the following day. With the way the heat never seemed to ease, Cinza grew convinced she was ill, but there was little she could do about it.

She was weak and weary when the first rattle came from the door. Blinking open bleary eyes to a dim shed, she pushed back her mass of grimy hair as she forced herself to sit up. She'd thought she'd be able to attempt getting free when Eevid returned, but whatever was burning through her combined with the minimal water and lack of food left her too weak.

Trying to keep her racing heart under control, Cinza waited as the scraping stopped and the lock clicked. It seemed like hours passed as the doors swung open, but Eevid wasn't on the other side staring back at her.

"Look at what we have here."

The shadow on the right stepped forward. With the sun already setting, there wasn't much light for her to see by, but she could guess what these men were without it.

Alphas.

Two of them, each more than twice her size, though she could see they didn't have wings. The dark skin of the one on the left made him harder to see amid the shadows in the shed as he moved forward, but their intent was obvious.

Crushing Cinza

They were there for her. Her stepmother had sold her, and these alphas had come to collect.

Cinza struggled to rise to her feet, to do *what* she wasn't sure, but the alpha who'd spoken reached her before her shaky legs could bear her weight. Grabbing her waist, he plastered her to his front, nose buried in her hair before she even had time to draw breath.

She screamed. A hand clamped over her mouth as a second body pressed to her back, trapping her wings. Sandwiched between the two males, there was no escape to be found.

Baring her teeth, she tried to bite the fingers blocking her scream but only earned a chuckle in response. The male kept his hand flat, leaving her nothing to sink her teeth into. Her struggles were only feeble twitches, allowing her to feel the excitement of the two alphas holding her.

"A little grubby, but nothing we can't fix. She smells divine," said the one at her back.

Though her stomach rolled and threatened to empty itself, Cinza's cheeks burned with shame when her body responded to the men's pheromones. Core clenching and nipples tightening into points, she denied the trickle of wetness between her thighs.

"I can't wait to sink myself into her wet cunt."

The growled words came with a nip to her throat, causing Cinza to whimper and fight harder to pull away. Tears leaked from the corners of her eyes as she strained to turn them to plead with the alphas, but the hand over her mouth kept her from finding either man's eyes.

"Are you going to be a good little omega?"

A growl rattled in Cinza's chest as she tried to bite the fingers once again. The men only laughed at her. All her self-defense training hadn't prepared her to take on two males, and her body wasn't responding as it should in her weakened state.

"C'mon, tie her hands so we can get going. She said the father doesn't return till late, but we don't want to be here too long."

Bitter horror flooded through Cinza as the male in front of her stepped back, catching her wrists when she tried to swing at him. His grip was bruising, morphing her growl into a whine of pain as he moved both of her hands to one of his and pulled something from his back pocket. The roughness threaded around her flesh told her it was rope, but his strength was too much for her to pull free.

Lifting a leg to kick out, he blocked her by pressing against her once again. With her hands tied in front of her, she couldn't flinch away when his erection settled between her forearms, and his lewd thrust had bile rushing up her throat.

"Fight all you want, sweetheart. Once we fill your sweet cunt a few times, you'll turn into our docile little pet. No bites and bonding for you. We want your heat to last."

Her shudder of revulsion brought more laughter as both men stepped back, the hand over her mouth staying in place as a second moved to grip her hair. The other alpha took her bound wrists, turning to pull her toward the door.

As brave as she tried to be, fear flooded her system, leaving her sucking great gasps of air over stubborn fingers. She worked to scream despite the hand, the sound so muffled she knew no one would hear, but she wouldn't accept defeat.

Batting her wings and kicking her legs, she twisted and fought, trying to get free of their hands. Growls and curses filled the surrounding air, but nothing she did worked. Pulled back against a hard chest yet again to make her wings useless, the alpha lifted her from her feet, ignoring her heels drumming against his shins.

"We're going to have to break her. Fast."

The alpha in front stopped just outside the doors of the shed, his gaze black.

"We can do it now. She won't have any fight left in her once we both mount her. Take both holes at once, and I doubt she'll move at all for a while."

His teeth glinted as he grinned, but she felt the alpha behind her shaking his head. A rush of relief cleared her mind, and for a moment she thought she caught a familiar scent.

"No time. She's not far enough along to take her roughly, and if we're caught, we're out of a lot of money."

The smile faded from the one in front of her, but he grunted an acknowledgment. Turning to lead the way once again, he called back over his shoulder.

"Then let's go. If she keeps kicking, we'll just tie her feet."

Trembling, Cinza let her body go limp. If they tied her feet, she'd truly be at their mercy. Her kicks were ineffective, so it was smarter to wait and hope something would give her the chance to run.

As the alpha carrying her stepped out into the night, she shook with the sudden desire to be back inside the shed after days of trying to escape. She did not know where they were taking her, but she knew what was coming. Dying alone in the shed would have been better.

Saying a silent prayer for a miracle, Cinza glared toward the house where she'd been nothing more than a servant. She'd repay everything Eevid had done to her.

Chapter 16

Armyn

He stared at the gaudy street sign and ran his fingers through his hair. When Luzor yelled his new address to him as he left, Armyn had nearly ripped his hair out in frustration.

There was nothing wrong with living in the posh community near the castle walls, but Cinza had never been interested in all the societal jockeying omegas her age seemed to thrive on. It was one thing that had drawn him to her. She'd been so adorably shy as a young girl, he'd been unable to resist the pureness of her heart. Yet now she lived exactly where the other girls had sought to live, in an overly ornate and well sought-after neighborhood. It was wrong.

The lights illuminated the sidewalk in a warm, gentle light, but unease crawled up Armyn's spine. Every house on the block had a brightly lit front porch, as well as many lights spilling out into the night from the interior of the home. Each one sported sheer curtains which hid enough of the inside to provide privacy but basic shapes were still visible. Almost every house had multiple people moving around inside it, so when Armyn approached the address Administrator Glashu had given him, he stopped.

Despite watching for several moments, no movement showed behind the few rooms with lights on. He almost stepped onto the path to the front door but paused when something alerted his senses.

Were Cinza's stepmother and stepsister still out in town so late at night, or had they simply settled for the night? The house seemed empty, so what had caught his attention?

He scanned the area before deciding to walk around the outside of the house to the backyard. After turning the corner, he noted how far apart even the backyard fences were between houses. The lights beside the road did nothing to brighten the side yards, which meant the back of the home would be close to pitch black on nights like tonight. With a sliver of moon hiding amid the twinkling stars, the clouds blocked what little illumination the heavens offered.

Stalking along the fence line, Armyn tucked his wings close and crouched, hearing a disconcerting noise.

It came again, the sound of muffled violence so out of place in the uppity neighborhood that his adrenaline skyrocketed. He spread his wings and launched himself over the gate, too impatient to even check if it was unlocked, his gut telling him Cinza was in trouble.

As he descended on the other side, he kept to the shadows in the back corner of the yard, avoiding the lush leaves of the tiny clump of bushes. As he settled his talons into the soft grass, he skimmed from one side of the house to the other before stalking to the edge of the tree line.

Standing in the deep shadow of the trees, he spotted the shed in the opposite corner, and calculated the distance between himself and the tiny building. He wondered why any single family would need so much outdoor space, then pulled his attention back to where it needed to be.

The sound came again, allowing him to pinpoint it as coming from within the tiny shack. Before he could dart forward to see what it was, the doors opened.

Out came a burly alpha, his stench so sour Armyn didn't need the breeze to carry it to him. He spoke to someone behind him. The clouds parted for a split second to reveal shiny, lustful eyes as he dragged slim wrists out from the darkness of the shed.

When Cinza's silvery blonde tresses shone in a moment of clear moonlight, Armyn lunged forward.

Another male held her back flush against his front, her dainty feet dangling a full foot off the ground as he manhandled her.

The sight of another alpha's fingers squeezing her breast colored his vision red.

With the aid of his wings, he sped toward them without sound, wanting nothing more than to rip her free of their touches before he annihilated them, but knowing she could get severely injured if he wasn't careful. Bunching his thigh muscles, he raised his right talon and gouged it into the first alpha's stomach as he swept past. He twisted his shoulder and extended his wing, slicing the male from shoulder to shoulder with his wingtip before tucking his upper extremities against his torso.

His talons dug into plush grass as he jerked himself to a stop, his airborne twist positioning him so he faced his prey. About six feet away from the bleeding alpha's side, he prepared to lunge forward and run the lethal tip of his wing across the man's trachea, only to stop as feminine sounds of pain rang in his ear.

The stench of alpha interest became swamped with the metallic scent of blood as the male he'd maimed sank to his knees and reached the ground in front of him. As the alpha tried to retrieve the entrails splatting onto the grass from his stomach, Armyn shot his gaze toward Cinza.

Her other assailant had set her on her feet and twirled her so she had to stare up into his angry face as he glared at Armyn, his thick fingers encasing her slender throat with ease.

Armyn froze in place, flexing his talons deeper into the dirt in case he needed to lunge but knowing he couldn't risk moving if the idiot was serious about snapping her neck. Meeting the tall, rounded, dark-skinned male's face, Armyn snarled.

"I'll kill her if you move any closer."

Before Armyn's growl left his chest, Cinza's tiny knee shot forward and embedded itself between the male's legs. Eyes popping wide in pain, the other alpha swung as he crumpled.

Cinza's face swiveled toward Armyn as the smack resounded through the night, her hair hiding her features as both prey and predator seemed to sink to the ground in slow motion. Thrusting as hard as he could with his wings, Armyn rocketed forward and flung his hand out, catching Cinza's head before her skull cracked against the concrete slab surrounding the shed.

As he belly-flopped onto the ground, Armyn grunted and flapped his wings, setting her head down gently before rising to his full height.

Her scent punched him in the nose, the raw heat and sweet cinnamon of her pheromones flooding his mouth with saliva. He wanted nothing more than to gather her close and ravage her, but the incoherent mumbling and wet, squishy sounds of the man he'd first attacked kept him in the present.

He slammed the other male's forearm down onto the concrete with his spread talons when the idiot reached for Cinza. The prince smirked in the darkness as the idiot wheezed and grabbed his ruined family jewels.

These were deaths he would never mourn. They'd planned to steal his omega. They'd hurt her. Laid their filthy hands on her.

The visceral, ruthless side of him basked in the fear shining up at him from his next victim. The poor brute knew he could count his last breaths on one hand.

Bloodthirsty and furious, Armyn settled his weight on the male's pinned arm. Even as part of him worried about Cinza's sensibilities, he couldn't stop himself from what came next.

His omega deserved nothing less than to be free of these lowlifes.

Permanently.

Chapter 17

Cinza

She stared at the alpha who was attempting to hold in his insides. A spreading pool of darkness surrounded him, and he swayed. As macabre as the sight was, Cinza couldn't look away until the male toppled to his side in the dirt.

A wet crunch came from her other side, and she lifted her head enough to turn it, spotting the second downed male. One taloned foot pinned a reaching arm while the other sank into the side of his skull.

Blood, pitch black in the darkness, welled around flexing toes. Gleaming bits of bone protruded in places while things she didn't want to name seemed to squish out in others.

Knowing what they'd planned for her kept any remorse at bay, but bile still rose in the back of her throat at the sight of a dangling eye pointed her way.

Cinza heaved, about to roll away from the gruesome sight, but stopped herself when she realized it would bring her closer to the other. She struggled to stand to get away but couldn't rise higher than a kneeling position. Strong hands reached under her arms, lifting her slight frame. They didn't stop after placing her on her feet, raising her clear off the ground until warm, sturdy arms cradled her and a familiar scent bathed her.

A scent laced with the metallic tang of blood in the air.

"Cinza."

Her name, spoken in such a gruff baritone voice, sent a shiver rocking her spine and guided her face up to meet a golden gaze. She'd hadn't trusted her eyes when Armyn arrived like an avenging angel, but she couldn't deny it, not with his arms wrapped around her.

Opening her mouth to speak, she stopped as a noise emerged from the street. Cinza stretched her neck and peered over Armyn's shoulder, squinting in the bright light emanating from every window in her house. The lights hadn't been on seconds ago, otherwise she wouldn't have been able to hold back her bile since the details of her attackers' deaths wouldn't have been hidden in darkness.

"Armyn! Prince!"

The call came from the back of the ostentatious place she called home, and Armyn turned to face the speaker. Cinza whimpered and snuggled into Armyn's arms on instinct, worried about the trouble he could face for rescuing her, but as the lights in the backyard turned on, she recognized her father's figure striding closer.

He paused when he came around a bush and noticed what littered the ground. Approaching with slow steps, she could see the tenseness in the set of his wings.

"Did you find her? Is that—"

He took a few rushed steps when her eyes met his, but he froze when Armyn's growl filled the space between them. Gaze lifting and brows rising, he stared over her head at the alpha clutching her tighter to his chest.

"Father or not, she's entering her cycle, and you won't come any closer."

She could see the flash of hurt and anger on her father's face, but he buried it, making a slow nod before his attention moved back to her.

"Cinza, are you hurt?"

Her throat rasped when she tried to speak, and she had to clear it before she could get any words out. The cramps in her belly were stronger, drowning out any other aches besides the need for water.

"I-I don't think so. Nothing permanent. Armyn got here in time."

Her father's eyes dropped to the mess surrounding them, his face pinched.

"What happened?"

He didn't look up as he asked, but the reminder sent a surge of strength through her as anger returned.

"Eevid happened. She locked me in the shed after the ball and sold me to these alphas. She confessed to—"

Cinza's breath caught, a sob threatening to choke off what she needed to say, but she refused to let another second pass without announcing Eevid's deeds.

"She confessed to killing Mother. She waited until I twirled to push the lid onto her back. I thought I'd killed her, but I didn't. It was Eevid."

Tears thickened her words, but she forced them out. Startled eyes lifted to hers, shock morphing to pain, followed by rage.

"You're sure?"

Her father's hands balled at his sides, his body practically vibrating with the anger she could feel radiating from him, and a small part of her rose and applauded. It was time he saw Eevid for what she was and avenged his true mate. She only wished she'd get to see it.

"She told me herself as she dragged me back here. She planned to kill me too, until I *proved useful* by doing chores. All the chores. She was going to poison me with suppressants and stage an overdose."

Agony filled her father's face as he gazed at her. He took a step forward before another snarl stopped him. His throat worked for a moment before he could say anything, and the words broke her heart anew.

"I'm sorry. I'm so sorry."

She wanted to put her arms around his neck and tell him it was okay, but Armyn held her tight, and she knew it wasn't the time to push him. Adrenaline still filled his system, flooding the surrounding air with his intoxicating scent.

"I know."

It was all she could say.

As others spilled from the back of their house, her father's attention turned away. He straightened as he glanced back toward them, fresh determination filling his face.

"I'll take care of whatever needs to happen here tonight. Eevid will pay for what she's done. You take care of my daughter."

The stare he pinned on Armyn seemed to carry unspoken words, and Cinza swiveled her head in time to see Armyn nod. Whatever passed between them, her father seemed satisfied that she was safe because he turned away to meet the guards moving through the yard.

Golden eyes tipped down to meet hers, and the hunger she could see there stole her breath. Brows furrowing, a look of pain crossed Armyn's face before he opened his mouth to speak, delivering another shock.

"Cinza, I'm sorry as well."

Her eyes widened as she stared up at her haughty prince, humbling himself with words she had doubted he would ever speak.

"I'm sorry for what I've done to you. For what's happened in my absence. For everything you've been through."

It took a moment for her to find her voice, her mind still reeling. Between the weakness trembling within her body and the effects of adrenaline withdrawing from her system, she was half convinced she was hallucinating.

"I think I'm in shock."

One brow lifted. His lips quirked to the side as she pressed her tied hands to her forehead.

"You're going to have to apologize again when I'm not on the verge of passing out. I'm not sure I believe this is real."

His chuckle rumbled against her side while he squeezed her tighter to his chest and shook his head. The world swayed as he stalked forward, but he wasn't walking toward her house.

"You're not the girl I thought you were, Cinza, but I'll apologize to you as many times as it takes."

She ignored the comment as she tried to figure out where he was taking her. Wiggling, she pushed at his arm.

"You can put me down now."

"I could."

He kept his gaze fixed over her head, focusing on whatever destination he'd chosen as he continued to carry her.

"And you could untie me."

She watched his smile widen before he looked down at her again. It was the expression she remembered from their childhood, the first genuine smile she'd seen since he'd returned.

"I know. But I don't want to."

A gasp ripped from her as he leaped into the air, wings snapping open to drive them higher. For a moment, the sight of the town growing smaller beneath them stole her ability to speak, but a harsh cramp brought her focus back.

"Where are you taking me? I need my room. My bed."

Another chuckle rolled through his chest as he shook his head. Wings turning, he spun them around, snatching her breath again as her stomach dropped.

"No, you don't. You need my den and my knot. You're going into heat, and I'm going to claim you."

Chapter 18

Armyn

Her cute little gasp morphed to a whine as another cramp tightened her midsection, the wind whisking away too much of her scent for his liking. He wanted to fill his lungs with her pheromones but opted to focus on the castle as it came into view instead, reining in his desire despite the adrenaline still coursing through him.

When his talons accepted both his and Cinza's weight, Armyn tucked his wings against his back and stalked across his private balcony. Since every light was on inside his bedchamber, he saw the two men cleaning the room.

Refusing to release his bundle of disheveled perfection, he rapped the glass with his wing and stepped back, waiting for the person closest to the door to come open it.

Cinza finally relaxed from the dastardly cramp, sucking in a relieved breath before turning stormy, luminescent eyes up to him.

The door opened at the same time her mouth did, silencing her when she realized they had company.

"Thank you, Jaylar. Now out. Both of you," Armyn demanded.

He barely refrained from snarling at the two beta men who'd tended his chambers for many years before he left for the military.

His mother had been wise to change the staff who cleaned and restocked his private rooms from female to male long before he'd hit puberty. For now, though, even the betas were too much. He needed solitude with his omega.

The men scrambled to the door, Jaylar turning to meet the prince's eyes to remind him they'd be available if he needed anything.

Hearing the door lock behind the beta helped lower his hackles as he kicked the balcony door shut behind him. After punching the key code with his wing to engage this lock as well, Armyn stepped further into his den, only to be elbowed by his future princess.

Her sharp joint dug between the ribs below his pectoral as she glared up at him.

"You can't just whisk me away and say things like that without asking me."

"I already have."

Cinza's lips thinned before they tightened as another cramp stole through her, this one blessedly short. The warm cinnamon perfume of her slick made him want to mount her on the floor where he stood.

She didn't recover from this cramp as well as she did the one before; her flushed cheeks in stark contrast with her pale flesh. With her head lolling on his bicep, she spoke with less fervor even as sparks flew from her blue orbs.

"Who says I want you?"

"Your body."

"But what if *I* don't? I can't do this, Armyn."

"Yes, you can, although it won't be easy. You've been on suppressants for a long time."

"What does—"

Her gasp of pain as another cramp seized her insides urged his feet forward. Before he'd gotten to the fully stocked sidebar, she'd gone lax in his arms again.

"What does that have to do with anything?"

"Everything. If I'd have protected you, you never would have taken a single pill, but since I wasn't here when you needed me most, you've been taking them for years. They're toxic, even lethal, if taken long-term, not just if you overdose."

Still limp in his arms, Cinza kept her gaze aimed at his chin while her brows furrowed. Unable to allow a single centimeter of space to separate them, Armyn squatted down with her in his arms and opened the built-in fridge in the fancy piece of furniture pressed against his wall. He shifted her around until the brunt of her weight rested on one of his arms and used the other to grab a plate of sliced fruits from the top shelf of the fridge. He stood, closed the fridge with his talon, and set the plate on the table before returning to the sidebar. Lifting a hatch, he yanked out a fat loaf of fresh bread. Taking the entire thing to the quaint little table, he tossed it down and turned yet again back to the sidebar.

"I'm not a doll. Set me down."

"No."

Despite her vehement words, she didn't fight his hold. When another cramp ravaged her womb, Armyn's worry shot his heart up into his throat.

Grabbing the entire jug of filtered water from the fridge, he hurried back to the little table and sat down, filling a glass with an inch of water.

Cinza's attention latched on to the crystal-clear cup, but when she lifted her hand to grab it, she scowled at her bound wrists. The throbbing in Armyn's throat indicated his heart did not enjoy watching the pain-filled emotions flashing through her features, even if his cock did.

"Please untie me."

He ignored her plea and lifted the glass to her lips. She closed her eyes and shook her head.

The cool cup under his fingers stopped him from squeezing it in frustration—he'd never forgive himself if he rained shards of glass down on her by shattering it in irritation. When he pressed it tighter against her mouth, she pierced his soul with her luminescent blues.

Armyn set the water back on the table, gritting his teeth as his growl relayed his emotions.

"Why won't you drink the water? Because I'm offering it?"

"N-no, I—"

Her body tried to ball up as another wave of pain scorched her insides, a tiny trickle of wetness seeping into his lap.

She should be dripping. Gushing. Creating a copious amount of slick to ease his entrance. Not the mere dribble that escaped.

Cinza needed water. Now.

"*Th-they* tied my wrists."

She shook within his arms, her ragged breathing and devastated eyes slicing his soul in two.

He purred for her. The vibration seeped into her form and dampened the fear and revulsion running rampant through her. He pulled his arm from under her legs and slid the knife out of the slim holster at his hip, slicing the rope before his next breath.

"I-I still smell them. I want to wash."

"We will, Cinza, but you need to drink first. Let me take care of you. Stop fighting me," Armyn said.

He'd never come so close to begging before.

This time when he lifted the glass to her lips, she didn't balk or try to reach for it, greedily gulping down the first bit before he could regulate her. When he lowered the glass to slow her so she didn't get sick, her dainty snarl pulled his lips up into a grin. He'd worried he'd broken her feistiness, but it was still there.

Knowing she was too desperate to listen to reason, Armyn tightened his arm around her and strengthened his purr, urging her to relax into his care. As Cinza sipped the liquid, her flesh went from cold to hot, almost as though he'd dunked her in boiling water instead of offering her a chilled beverage.

She whimpered as every drop seemed to arrow straight to making more slick, her overdue body frantic to expel the heats she'd refused it. Armyn quickly poured her another inch, watching as her plump lips pressed against the cup.

More slick dampened his lap, but it still wasn't nearly enough. When the second small cup of water stayed in her belly, he leaned forward and grabbed a piece of fruit.

She shook her head and reached for the glass, but Armyn hooked his forearm over her elbow and forced her limb back to her side with the arm he used to support her back. Despite her look of frustration, Cinza ate the berry he offered her.

Alternating between small bites of food and sips of water, Armyn fed Cinza from his hand until she squirmed in his lap. He picked up the cup, but she wrapped her delicate digits around his wrist and shook her head.

He almost made her drink it anyway, but the silent plea shining from her wide eyes stayed his hand.

"I'm ready to shower."

"I thought you'd never ask. I can't wait to strip you."

Her mouth popped open and disbelief colored her cheeks.

"I meant alone!"

He smirked as he stood, rubbing his cheek on the top of her head. When he carried her to the bathroom and kicked the door shut behind them, she squeaked a protest only to gasp as he set her rear on the frigid marble countertop. No doubt her wet clothes soaked up the cold, shocking her heated intimates.

Armyn pinned her knees to the edge of the vanity with his hipbones, unapologetic of the turgid length attempting to escape his trousers.

Cinza made another cute, startled sound as he peeled his vest off his shoulders and shook his wings, tossing it onto the ground. The golden buttons clinked against the stone as Armyn shucked his undershirt over his head, ripping the ties which once secured it around the base of his wings. He met Cinza's wide eyes as the material slipped from his fingers and whispered to the floor.

Her focus dipped to his bared chest as though pulled by a magnet, a groan passing between her lips as another cramp wrecked her insides. When the wave passed, she slumped against the mirror behind her, her wings spreading to cling to the reflective surface as tears filled her lashes.

Armyn cupped her cheek in his palm, spearing his fingertips into her dirty locks and purring a comforting note.

"It *hurts,* and you smell so good."

She didn't seem to realize she'd spoken aloud until his lips tilted in a grin and his free hand busied itself with unfastening the front of her bustier. He quickened his movements as another spasm tightened her abdomen, her muscles quivering under his knuckles as he popped the last hook loose. Wanting nothing more than to push the material off her shoulders and press his face between her pert breasts, he deepened his purr and stroked her cheek with his thumb. With monumental effort, Armyn denied himself the urge and instead continued downward, unbuttoning her skirt and reaching through the opening to unsnap the sheer petticoat underneath.

The pale flesh showing through her open clothes made his mouth water and his cock jerk within his pants. As her eyes cleared and her breathing regulated, Armyn forced his gaze to meet hers.

"You're mine, Cinza. You always have been. It's time for me to prove it."

A tear escaped her lower lashes, trailing down until it pooled against his hand. Even as she shook her head in denial, she soaked up his purr and arched into the finger he trailed down her sternum. When he reached her lowest rib, he traced it, brushing her top to the side and revealing her gorgeous breast.

Her turgid nipple begged for his attention, but Armyn drew out their torture, running his finger along her rib in the other direction. As the fabric slipped off her left breast, her nipples darkened and peaked further, her ragged breathing making the mounds shudder.

With her bustier puddling on the counter under her, she looked like a goddess too pure for the likes of him, even with his lineage. His breath caught in his chest, interrupting his purr as he stood staring in awe.

Cinza shifted as though she intended to cover her breasts, but Armyn captured her wrists and transferred them both to one hand. Pinning them to his chest, he wrapped his other fingers around her nape and lifted her into a sitting position.

Leaning down until her breath wafted across his lips, Armyn paused and resumed his purr, loving the way she leaned closer.

Somehow, he ran his tongue along her lower lip but didn't invade her sweet mouth the way he longed to.

"These are the last lips I'll kiss, Tiny. After your sweetness, I couldn't stand the thought of kissing anyone else."

Her gasp drew him in, his control snapping as his tongue delved between her teeth and explored her depths so thoroughly, they both fought for breath when he pulled back. Another cramp began, so Armyn ducked his head down and reclaimed her mouth, hoping to distract her from the pain. She whimpered and writhed, prompting him to release her wrists and guide her palms to explore his chest.

His fingers slid down her abdomen and snuck under the waistband of her skirt, not stopping until he found the swollen bundle of nerves at the top of her sex.

Dainty fingers wrapped around his wrist even as her legs parted and her hips bucked.

She shattered after a few gentle strokes, her cry blocked by his mouth as he tangled his tongue with hers. Armyn nipped her bottom lip and slid his hand out of her skirt when she went limp with relief.

He propped her back against the mirror again while he filled a cup with water from the sink. She drank it from him without qualms, her dazed orbs spearing pride and worry through his veins.

When he stepped back and stripped himself of his pants, her inhale bounced off the walls.

Sensing her reprieve would only last a few minutes, Armyn grabbed her wrists and urged her to stand. He watched as her skirts seemed to fall in slow motion, revealing the sexiest body he'd ever seen, despite how thin she'd grown from neglect. He knew she'd blossom again under his care.

Her squeak endeared her to him more, yanking a groan from his chest. Since he refused to release her wrists, there was nothing she could do to cover herself, which left her completely nude to his hungry gaze.

Lust threatened to consume his every thought, but the lingering pheromones of foreign alphas pulled him toward the shower.

She stood awkwardly in the huge enclosure while he shut the door and chose the settings, but she didn't fight or try to get away, which made hope grow behind Armyn's breastbone. When warm water sprayed from the entire ceiling of the shower, she stiffened in shock before relaxing and letting out a sigh. Armyn pulled her front flush against his, unable to deny himself the pleasure of feeling her wet flesh rub against him, but he ran his fingers along her scalp to prevent himself from exploring every inch of her body.

He wanted to roar as the soap cycle began and carried the scent of her slick down the drain, yet he felt relief when the stench of the other alphas disappeared.

Cinza whimpered as another wave of heat began in her core. Armyn turned her around by her shoulders and plastered her back against his front, reaching between her legs to ease her with another orgasm. Her hands shot up, one grabbing his wrist while the other dug her nails into his bicep.

"Let me ease you, Cinza."

"It *hurts*."

Water replaced the soap, leaving nothing but their fresh pheromones and steam swirling through the air.

He stroked her clit with relentless fingers until she tilted her hips, silently asking for more. Unable to resist the call of her omega needs, he dipped two fingers lower.

She rose onto her tiptoes when he pressed them against her entrance, her whimper one of pain and desire. Even with her slick coating his digits, he couldn't wedge both in, so he eased one into her tight heat and worked it in and out until she clamped around him.

The water shut off just in time for him to enjoy the sound of her slick splashing onto the floor.

Taking advantage of her relaxed post-orgasm haze, he added a second finger and kept pushing them into her until his palm lay flush against her mound.

His cock leaked against the small of her back, adding his robust pheromones to her tempting cinnamon. For long, monumental seconds, neither of them moved.

His jaw ached from gritting his teeth, and his knot pulsed with the need to expand. But no matter how much he longed to sink into her depths, Armyn knew he had to tread carefully.

His Cinza deserved every nicety an omega could have, which meant mountains of blankets and a loving alpha.

Good thing he had both covered, even if her concept of "loving" far differed from his own.

Chapter 19

Cinza

With a hazy mind as Armyn's fingers left her core, Cinza's legs threatened to give out before he wrapped a thick arm around her waist to support her. Hands moving over her skin, he turned her to face him before pushing her back a step.

It was all she could do not to whine at the loss as he held her hips and the air cycle kicked on to dry them. As soon as the fan shut off, she leaped forward, plastering her chest to his stomach and wrapping her arms around his waist.

It was all too much. Eevid's confession, being trapped in the shed, the other alphas, Armyn's arrival… Her mind had whirled as they arrived in his suite, but as her cycle dragged her deeper into instincts, the only thoughts left were of the alpha standing before her.

A large hand cupped the back of her head, her hair still damp but at least not dripping. Cinza didn't bother to open her eyes as she felt Armyn bend, his lips crashing into hers before his tongue swept inside to steal what breath she had left.

The next cramp that rolled through her had tears pricking the back of her eyes. Her hip bones felt as though they were being crushed and drawn into her womb, fresh wetness spilling down her thighs as she broke away from the kiss to let out a cry.

She'd never expected heat to be like this, but she'd denied it so long her body seemed determined to make her feel the last few years' worth of pain all at once. When she pried her eyelids open, Armyn stared down at her, concern filling his usually arrogant face.

He lifted her into his arms without a word, tucking his wings close to carry her through the door, back into his bedchamber. The giant mattress occupying the alcove drew her gaze, but the gaudy gold blankets pulled a snarl from her chest as he moved closer to it.

"What's wrong?"

The rumbled question barely pierced the rage flooding her consciousness, and Cinza kicked her feet to be put down. Armyn resisted at first, but when she raked her nails over his forearm, he finally relented and set her on her feet.

In three steps, she clenched the horrid comforter in her hand. The thing was so heavy it took more effort than expected to remove it from the bed, but she finally wrestled it to the floor, giving it a disgusted kick before turning back to glare up at Armyn.

Arms crossed over his chest, he stared down at her with one brow raised. The corner of his lips twitched like he fought a smile, and her eyes narrowed.

"If you expect me to have my heat here, I want better bedding. Now."

The smirk escaped his control, gold irises flashing as his pupils flexed. She knew her pheromones affected him, but he was holding onto his urges better than she was.

"Whatever you wish, princess."

Her lip curled in a silent snarl before Cinza turned her back to him. Closing the space between herself and the bed, she ran a hand over the sheet still covering the mattress, humming at the feel. It was soft, but that wasn't what drew her to it. Leaning closer, she sucked in a deep breath, Armyn's spicy scent rising from the fabric to coat the back of her throat. Beneath the overt scent of him, there were traces of musk, but she found no hint of females.

Satisfied, she crawled up onto the mattress. It was so massive she could stretch out at the foot of the bed and there would still be enough room above her for another person her size, then another at each side. It was the most ridiculously luxurious thing she'd ever seen, and a part of her preened at the thought that her alpha was giving her such a lavish place to nest.

Her mind stuttered at those thoughts, but another cramp tore through her belly and scattered her worries. She was here now, and Armyn could help her through her heat. She'd worry about the rest later.

Cinza crawled forward until she found the place in the center where his scent was strongest, basking in the spot until a scrape nearby had her shooting upright. Armyn stood at the side of the bed, arms loaded with more thick blankets, his ruddy cock jutting out beneath them and stealing her attention. Her tongue escaped without conscious thought, nostrils flaring as she tried to catch the scent of his virility.

Shuffling closer on her knees, she almost growled when he set the blankets down in front of him, hiding her prize from view. She dragged them out of the way so she could explore him, but her fingers sinking into the plush linen distracted her. Releasing a soft hum, she clutched it to her face and smelled the fabric, rubbing her cheek over it in approval.

She looked around as she turned to find the best place for the blanket, brow furrowing as she realized she still didn't have enough to create the nest she'd imagined. She may not have built one since she was a small child playing with her mother, but there was a firm image in her mind of what it should be like.

Turning her head back to Armyn, she ignored the tightening of her core as her fingers continued to stroke the fabric clutched to her.

"More."

His brow tipped up, but he gave her a nod before striding off. She didn't pay attention to where he went, her mind focusing on where she was going to put everything. Crawling to the head of the bed, she gathered the pillows before backing into the middle of the mattress, deciding how she wanted to lay them.

She was still working when he returned, but she spared him a glance and nodded to where she wanted the blankets before making her next demand.

"Pillows."

His eyes narrowed, but she went back to fluffing the blankets and layering them the way she wanted. She fell into instinct, blocking out all thoughts until she'd wedged in the extra pillows and was ready to build the canopy, tipping her eyes to the alpha waiting beside the bed. He may be the male she'd always pictured in her nest, but his size still made her heart stutter and her womb throb. He was larger than he'd been when she'd first started dreaming of such things.

Scooting back until she was at the foot of her nest, she pointed to the center.

"Lay down."

Armyn's face remained neutral, but his cock bobbed at her order. His tip leaked a delicious scent into the air, but her omega urges demanded she focus on her task. The cramps no longer ripped through her, acting more like background tension than an all-consuming pain, giving her room to complete her nest so he had a secure place to soothe her desires.

Her eyes narrowed when Armyn didn't immediately obey, but she relaxed when he raised a knee to the bed. His gaze stayed locked on hers as he crawled closer, the gold almost lost to the black pits his pupils had become. She panicked when he crossed the edge of the nest, fearing he'd destroy what she'd created, but he was careful to climb over the ring of blankets and pillows to lie in the open center she'd left for him.

His wings took up so much space, there was no room for her beside him in the nook, but that didn't matter. Cinza planned to spend most of her time under him, yearning to have his broad shoulders blocking out the world.

Once Armyn settled, she crawled forward, straddling his legs as she turned to face his talons so she could weave their cocoon closed overtop them. She left it loose so there was room to move and shift, but only the upper portion of the nest would remain open to accommodate their wings.

Cinza shuffled backward as she worked, careful of Armyn's feathers as she moved yet so intent on her masterpiece she startled when large hands gripped her backside.

"You keep waving it in my face and I'm going to be forced to do something."

His rough, growl-laced voice forced a shiver up her spine. Her eyes dropped to the length bobbing below her chest, the tip glistening. His scent filled her nostrils, making her mouth water and her chest rumble.

Her head dipped lower as she nuzzled the side of his length, smearing wetness on her cheek as her eyes rolled back. With the need to create a safe space eased, the smell of him brought forth a new hunger.

Her hand slipped from the blanket to cup the heavy sac resting between his legs. She rolled it in her palm as Armyn released a growl that shuddered through her belly, calling fresh slick to coat her folds and drip onto his chest.

Tongue extending to lap at the length of him, she lost her treat before she truly got a taste; masculine fingers yanking her further back and forcing her knees wide around Armyn's torso. She clawed at the bed to drag herself back down until a warm mouth landed on her lower lips.

Freezing in place, Cinza's breath caught as Armyn's tongue swiped between her folds, catching the little pearl at the top of her crease with a twitch-inducing flick. The sound emerging from his chest was somewhere between a growl and a purr, melting her bones and leaving her flattened to his muscles as his hands canted her hips to get better access.

He devoured her.

Tongue lapping, lips pulling, teeth nibbling, he left no part of her sex untouched, the sounds of his approval rumbling into her body as she panted atop him. Tension curled tighter in her belly as her knees clamped to his sides, and she cried out when he finally sent her over the edge. Eyes clenched shut, white light searing her retinas, she twitched and shuddered atop him as new sensations washed through her limbs.

When her eyelids finally agreed to blink open, Armyn's cock stood in front of her face. Angry red and throbbing, rivulets of tempting fluid ran down the length, calling her to take what she craved. Though Armyn still licked at the slick on her thighs, she took hold of his shaft and pulled herself down until she could fit the head in her mouth. Moaning as his flavor burst on her tongue, she scooted further until he hit the back of her throat before pulling off and running her tongue down to the base.

Her core fluttered with want, but she needed to taste more of him.

Taking him into her mouth again, her hand worked the length she couldn't fit, coaxing the alpha to spill his seed to feed her. He was still at first, but as she suctioned her lips around him and wriggled her tongue, he moved his hips, thrusting up as she bobbed down, forcing her to take more and more.

Armyn stiffened further under her attentions, growing impossibly thicker. Her fingers found where his knot would expand, kneading the place to the sound of his hiss.

Blunt digits traced her entrance as Armyn's hips rocked faster before one dipped inside her channel. He pumped twice before adding a second, then worked to fit in a third.

"I'm going to fill your pretty mouth, Cinza, and I'm going to stuff your pussy too, so fly apart as you drink me down."

She moaned around the pulsing flesh in her mouth, her entire focus on the sensation of his fingers moving inside her and the taste of him on her tongue. His thrusts came faster, both with his hand and his hips, filling her from both ends at the same time. Her own orgasm rose as his movements grew erratic, the flexing of his shaft warning her he was close.

As the first pulse of his seed hit the back of her throat, he shoved in a fourth finger, his knuckles stretching her entrance. She choked on her cry as he flooded her mouth, the wave of decadent fluid forcing her to swallow or release her prize.

Sucking on his tip as shudders rocked through her body, Cinza drank down every drop, fresh heat blooming in her belly as his offering settled in her stomach and soothed some of her need. Her core still demanded more, but for the moment, she was content.

As Armyn's release trickled off, he pulled himself from her mouth, sitting up to lift and turn her so she faced him as she rested on his chest. His deep breaths raised her up and down, the sound of his heart pounding beneath her ear calming her and leaving her in a daze as his hands moved along her body.

When his cock twitched against the inside of her thigh, she raised shocked eyes to meet his, the smirk on his face one she'd seen so many times.

"Sweet, perfect omega. There's still more."

As tired as she felt, her core clenched at the promise in his words, awakening with new demand. Her heat wouldn't end until her alpha knotted and seeded her, her body demanding more until it received what it needed.

She dug her fingers through the downy feathers as she pushed herself up. The tip of him nestled between her cheeks, scorching her flesh and drawing forth a wave of fresh slick.

"Then knot me, Armyn."

Chapter 20

Armyn

He had dreamed about this moment for years, even told himself he was a fool for idolizing and yearning for one woman when he could have anyone, but now that the moment was happening, her perfection blew Armyn away.

Never in a million years had he imagined his sweet, innocent, shy omega would say such words, especially in such a demanding voice.

He loved it, his cock jerking along her folds and his smirk widening into a smile.

He'd love torturing her into a mass of wordless, writhing need, too.

Grasping her hips and thrusting his length against her pussy, Armyn reveled in her moan.

Slick replaced his saliva as he teased himself along her folds.

Cinza's hips took up his rhythm, grinding with enthusiasm and testing his control. To draw her deeper into lust, Armyn kept one hand clasped around her hip, limiting her movement, and trailed his other up her torso. Her delectable breast fit in the palm of his hand, making his mouth water for a proper taste, but he soothed himself by plucking her nipple and promising himself he'd pamper her into a fuller figure for her next heat. The ribs he felt beneath the pillowed flesh left him worried he'd be too rough and damage her.

She whimpered and groaned, her spine undulating as she tried to break his grip on her hip.

"Armyn, please."

"I love it when you beg."

Shifting his hand to play with her other breast, Armyn enjoyed the flush blooming on her torso and filling her cheeks. Her pupils had swallowed her irises, and although he loved her luminescent orbs, he couldn't help but fall even deeper under her spell as he stared up into her dark gaze. She looked like a woman unhinged, her pupils blown and her hair falling around her shoulders while she ground herself against him.

He couldn't bear it any longer. Unable to wait another second, Armyn flipped them over. Mindful of her beautiful nest, he made sure his wings didn't spread until he cleared the mounds of fabric.

He fitted his tip to her sopping entrance and pressed into her, both of them groaning when he sank an inch into her opening. His purr vibrated from his chest, helping Cinza relax despite another wave of desire cramping her core. Slick drenched their thighs as Armyn ruthlessly pushed forward, drowning in both her tight sheath and her expressive eyes.

Her gasp as he surged forward, cramming his last few inches into her, snapped his control. Seed spurted from his cock as he drew his hips back just enough to deny her his knot. He wasn't ready for this to be over just yet.

His head darted forward, burying his teeth into her shoulder and staking his claim over her heart. Cinza's squeal cut short, leaving nothing but his groan to fill the air until her sob arrowed through him.

Armyn extracted his teeth from her flesh and licked the wound, pushing away the urge to hum in delight over her taste. Worry twisted in his guts even though his release coated her insides as her breath hitched.

His half-formed knot hated the cool air, pulsing in want of her tight body, but he pulled back and met her gaze.

With her channel bathed in his release and the orgasms he'd previously given her, Cinza's need was low enough to allow her to think beyond her instincts. The side of her fist thumped against his breastbone, and agony shone from her leaking eyes.

"Why? Why did you mark me?"

"I told you I would. You're mine."

His words only increased whatever emotions she held, her tears flowing almost as freely as her slick.

Armyn couldn't stop his hips from surging his cock in and out of her, rage building behind his sternum with every angry thump of her fist against it.

"You also said you'd fuck and discard me, so I can't believe anything you say!"

Armyn froze at both her remark and the anguish filling her face. He searched his memory, uncertain where she'd gotten those words. So much had happened so quickly. He'd forgotten how badly he'd treated her before he left. The memory of her hopeful yet agonized expression as he walked away from her all those years ago came flooding back, along with the flippant words he'd given her.

But hadn't he already proven things weren't the same? She'd been his guiding light for almost a decade, ruled his dreams when he was neck deep in enemy territory, kept him sane as he resisted torture.

Hadn't he killed two men to save her? Helped expose the horrible woman who'd mistreated her for years?

With half his heart beating in her chest, she'd be able to see how desperate he was for her. All she had to do was look past her pain and she'd know how much he needed her. How long he'd been in love with her.

Yet she fought him, even now, with his cock invading her cunt and her body desperate for more.

When her name left him in a stern, warning tone, she shuddered underneath him but turned fiery eyes up to his.

She gritted her teeth in a mutinous expression as another cramp began low in her abdomen.

Armyn snarled and yanked his cock all the way out of her, only to thrust and bury himself to the hilt. When her insides tightened in relief, he left the haven of her body and hovered above her.

"You're mine. Forever. There's no changing it now."

She said nothing, crying through clenched teeth as he denied her.

Furious she'd refute his claim, Armyn grabbed her hair and pinned her hip to the mattress with his other hand.

"Mark me," he demanded, lowering his neck and pressing it against her mouth.

She refused, lips tight.

Snarling, Armyn snapped his hips forward, burying his cock so deep inside her his groin ground against her clit before he yanked himself away again.

"Claim me," Armyn growled into her hair, his soul's turmoil growing with every passing second.

She shook her head, causing her soft lips to brush against his neck. His cock spurted over her eager opening, making her legs twitch around his hips, but still she refused.

Tightening his fist in her hair, he growled and pushed her into the mattress, pummeling his thick length in and out of her with such force he hit something spongy and soft deep within her. Her mouth popped open on a silent scream as he rammed into her harder and harder, yet she refused to bite down despite the scrape of her teeth on his flesh.

Infuriated, Armyn left her magnificent sheath and forced himself to release her. Sitting back on his heels, his breaths rattled in his chest as a band tightened around his heart.

She lay sprawled where he left her, her breasts heaving as she silently sobbed.

"I need you, Cinza. Me. Not as a prince, or a soldier, but *me*. My heart belongs to you—it always has. I'm an alpha, an asshole, arrogant, whatever you want to call me, but the truth remains."

With tightly controlled movements, he reached down and cupped her cheek in his palm.

"I can't live without you. I love you. I've always loved you."

His words were thick with both his repentant purr and his tears, the beauty under him stealing chunks of his soul without even trying.

Her brows shot up and her mouth popped open, her chest jerking to a halt as she searched his face.

"But... why?"

The lack of confidence in her tone shattered his soul, the realization of how deep he'd wounded her during their youth heaping guilt upon his conscience.

"Because there isn't an ounce of deceit in you. I grew up surrounded by power-hungry adults and conniving females who pursued me for their own purposes, but you... you were innocence personified. Pure and sweet, never looking for anything but love, and offering more forgiveness than anyone deserved. I couldn't resist—still can't resist—the lure of you. I'll do anything for you."

She wrapped her arms around herself in an uncertain hug, no doubt feeling the turmoil in their unfinished bond. Heat grew in her womb, her slick washing away the cum he'd used to soothe the worst of her estrous, and her nipples beaded above her slim arms as she stared up at him.

"Y-you won't go looking for another female as soon as my heat ends? You won't cast me aside?"

Armyn rested his forehead against hers and spoke the truth.

"Never. I'm never letting you go. There's no one else I'll ever want. Mark me as yours for the world to see."

She shuddered under him, the worry melting from her form before a sudden cramp had her crying out. Her dainty fingers grabbed his nape and hauled him closer, guiding his neck between her teeth.

Her hips wiggled under his, calling forth his need to rut and own this tiny bundle of perfection, so he thrust into her and seated himself as deep as her body would allow.

Lava boiled from his balls and shot from his tip as his knot locked behind her pubic bone and her teeth sank into his flesh, completing their bond. The world sparked to kaleidoscopic perfection as their hearts melded together, his soul pulsing with joy as hers joined it.

When she tore her teeth from his flesh and licked her mating mark, he reveled in the viciousness of it, wanting more, but when she met his gaze, her features relaxed and she smoothed her hand against the side of his face.

A drop of liquid landed on her cheek. Another followed.

"I love you too, Armyn. Despite all the reasons you gave me not to."

His chest shook with more than his purr, the pleasure coursing through his cock no competition for the happiness flowing through their bond. With his next heartbeat, he realized the drops falling onto her face were his tears.

He didn't mind them. They seemed appropriate for such an intense moment.

Cinza pulled him down for a kiss more profound than anything he'd experienced in his life.

Chapter 21

Cinza

"You need to eat."

The rough words tried to drag her from the sleep she so desperately wanted. Rolling onto her side, Cinza pulled the pillow over her head.

"I know you're tired, but you need food and water. Up."

Armyn punctuated his command by yanking the pillow away, but Cinza only burrowed further into her nest, using the blankets to block out the light.

"Go away."

She knew he heard her despite her slurred words. She had a few seconds of peace where she thought he might actually let her rest before the mattress dipped at her side. A hand gripped her shoulder, flattening her to the bed before his weight settled atop her hips.

"You've given me no choice."

The words came in a low warning seconds before fingertips dug into her bare sides. Sliding and seeking, they moved until they found the spots that made her body jerk in reaction, her eyes popping open to mimic her mouth as she cried out.

"Armyn! What? Stop!"

A broad grin covered his face as he stared down at her, his devilish fingers continuing to tickle. His wings mantled above them, giving him the appearance of some mischievous god bent on tormenting her with too much sensation.

"Please!"

She tried to roll and wiggle away, but his weight on her hips pinned her in place. She couldn't escape, and as she gasped for breath, she realized she didn't want to.

This was where she belonged.

Armyn finally relented, pausing his fingers. He kept them in place as she sucked in air laced with their scents. She could feel his excitement coursing through the bond, matched only by her joy, but there was a current of worry beneath it.

"I've got to get you healthy for my coronation. Can't have people thinking I neglect my omega."

She wiped the tears from her eyes before what he said clicked.

"Coronation? Already?"

Worry stirred in her chest, but he reached out to push the hair back from her face and soothe her.

"It's tradition to crown the prince when he returns from duty, but we have a few weeks before the ceremony. And father will still be here to guide me. We'll announce our wedding once I'm officially in power, then we'll say our vows and crown you as queen."

Her heart stuttered. The air froze in her lungs at his pronouncement. She may have grown up around the pomp and ceremony of royalty, but she'd never expected to be part of it. She'd studied foreign relations hoping to help her father one day, not to find her own place in the hierarchy.

"C-crown?"

Armyn leaned down to nuzzle his mark on her neck, tongue slipping out to send sparks of pleasure through her body.

"Of course. As my queen and consort. You'll rule at my side and soften my edges. Keep me in line."

The whispered words had warmth spreading through her even as a shiver of fear raced down her spine. Could she handle the demands of being Queen?

Armyn must have felt her trepidation because he pulled back to gaze down into her eyes. Thumb stroking her cheek, he pressed a quick kiss to her lips.

"You'll be a wonderful queen. You're caring and thoughtful. And forgiving."

He buried his nose against his mark again, leaving little kisses on her skin.

"I don't deserve your forgiveness after the pain I've caused you. I only hope I can earn it and prove my loyalty to you."

She raised her hands to run fingers through his hair, pulling him up to meet her gaze.

"I forgive you, Armyn. You don't have to earn anything. I've always seen the true you, even though you hide it from the world."

Tension left his face with her words, a burst of love flooding through their bond. She never expected to have what she'd dreamed of with Armyn, and she knew there would still be parts of their life that would be rocky, but for the first time since her mother's death, she could see a happy future.

"Now, up. You must eat."

She let out a squeal as the world flipped, Armyn somehow lifting her from the bed and tossing her over his shoulder as he straightened. She thrashed as he shuffled to the edge of the mattress before stepping off to carry her to the small table in one corner.

Her world spun again as Armyn deposited her on one of the two chairs before dropping into the one across from her with his typical smirk. A laden tray filled the table between them, and she had to admit the aromas rising from it made her mouth water and her stomach awaken.

"My first edict as Queen shall be to ban tickling and carrying me around like a sack. And any other high-handedness you might think to try."

Leaning forward, Armyn plucked a roll from the tray, lifting it to hold in front of her lips. It was the same type of roll he'd caught her stealing so long ago, and his eyes danced as he met her narrowed ones.

"Then I guess you'll just have to settle for Consort, and I'll rule all by myself," he stated as he pushed the roll forward. Mouth parted to nibble a corner, Cinza wasn't expecting the way he crammed the sticky mound toward her, smearing her lips and cheeks with sweetness.

He released the roll caught between her teeth, leaving it lodged there. Sliding from the chair to kneel before her as she tore off the piece in her mouth, mumbling obscenities around the dough, he caught her wrists and bent forward to take a bite from the piece clutched in her fingers.

A wicked golden gaze held her still as he leaned closer to lick her lower lip, sucking it into his mouth.

Life with Armyn wouldn't be easy. He was reckless and headstrong, but he was also honorable and loyal. He had duties that would always come first, but she knew he'd do everything he could to make her happy.

Cinza couldn't wait to do the same for him, eager to enjoy his devilish smirk at every opportunity.

And if it also meant she'd get his knot during her heats and his broad shoulders in her nest every night, then she'd happily be his queen.

Forever.

Chapter 22

Armyn

It wasn't a pleasant endeavor, but Armyn knew Cinza needed the closure before she could move on to the next part of their lives. He squeezed his omega's hand as the gavel struck, pronouncing Eevid guilty of murder.

Armyn held in his smirk as a wave of satisfaction hit him from his bond. Cinza's vindictiveness was nowhere near as tame as she let on. Yet no matter how much she agreed with the verdict, she didn't hate the woman—her grieving for her mother was too great. She had no room for hatred in her gentle heart, despite the horrible things she'd suffered.

Armyn had plenty of hate for the horrible woman, the woman's shameless daughter, and the vile enemies his solar system fought who had wrought so much damage on his team.

Fate wanted him and Cinza together—her goodness matched his darkness. Her softness fit perfectly against his hardness. Her gentle soul eased his violent tendencies.

Wrapping her arm around his, Armyn stood and walked down the courtroom's aisle, escorting his princess from the room before the juror read the punishments aloud. Cinza didn't need whatever self-imposed guilt she'd heap on herself whenever she learned the harsh fate of her tormentor.

Taking an immediate left when they exited the judicial room, Armyn took advantage of her distracted thoughts and shoved her into the fancy washroom, locking the door behind him.

Her squeak filled his heart with mischievous joy.

"You will *not* knot me in the bathroom."

Her glare did nothing to stop him. Propping her ass on the edge of the sink and dropping to his knees, Armyn smirked up at her as she gasped. He flipped her skirt up and tucked her knees over his shoulders, giving her no choice but to brace her hands on the sink so she didn't fall.

"You're right. I won't knot you in the bathroom. But you'll wish I had."

After using his teeth and tongue and lips to drive her over the edge several times, uncaring of who heard them, Armyn scooped up his princess and carried her limp form to their chambers.

She shot him a bemused glance when she saw their private quarters were teaming with servants, the entire castle full of scurrying workers getting things ready for his coronation. Her flushed cheeks and desperate eyes were enough of a consolation for the ache between his thighs.

Several hours later, he stood on the king's dais, staring out at the gathered representatives of his kingdom. He'd worked toward this moment his entire life, but it would have felt hollow if it weren't for the tiny omega sitting in the front row with her father.

As the ceremony came to a close and the imposing golden crown settled on his head, Armyn only had eyes for Cinza. Her luminescent blues outshone every gown in the palace, filling his soul with purpose and light.

The crowd broke into boisterous applause, his father's nod of pride and satisfaction straightening Armyn's spine. The years he'd spent in the military to earn this right had been difficult, but it taught him the discipline he'd lacked, and he knew he could lead his people better for it.

Sweeping his gaze across the attendees, the new king of Allhert met his dearest friends' eyes and expressed his gratitude without words.

Blaide stood at the side of the room with his arm resting across his mate's shoulders, tugging her close as their tails twined and danced behind them. The younger alpha's nod started Armyn's smile, their comradery bridging the space between them until it felt like they hadn't spent a day apart.

Ursuli sat in the front row with his omega placed strategically in the last chair, meaning no one else crowded her. The mermaid's vibrant skin and scales nearly glowed next to Ursuli's dark suit and darker skin, and as he pulled her closer, her alpha offered Armyn a rare grin.

Two of his closest friends understood the beautiful dance between alpha and omega.

The third? He stood in the darkest corner, his face tight with tension.

Armyn searched Quasim's face, his concern growing with every second the male avoided his gaze, though Quasim gave a nod of acknowledgment. He'd given Quasim the space he'd requested, glad his best friend hadn't had to suffer the admin side of the military, but his silence seemed to mark a worsening in his condition, not the healing Armyn had hoped for.

It seemed he'd been wrong to leave him alone for so long. Murky black orbs met his eyes, the drop into panic too close for Quasim to hide it from Armyn. They'd grown up together, gone on countless missions together, and yet the male sought to hide the misery lurking within his soul.

His best friend needed help. Armyn wouldn't let him down again.

Turning and settling on the throne, Armyn took his rightful place as ruler of his family's kingdom, the weight of duty already resting heavy on his shoulders.

He had so much to accomplish. So many responsibilities. Too many for just one person.

Extending his arm to Cinza, the first thing he did as king was pull his omega into his lap and announce his wedding plans. He was only giving them a month to prepare, too impatient to wait any longer to make her his queen.

The entire kingdom celebrated as he devoured Cinza's sweet lips. Her outrage at the display melted as he stroked her tongue with his, blasting his love through their bond.

He'd found happily ever after. Cinza had too, even if it had taken her longer to admit it. Their bond told him everything he needed to know.

He loved her. She loved him.

Just like in fairytales.

Epilogue

Quasim

Bitterness filled his mouth.

As his best friends found their perfect happily ever afters, Quasim rotted in the shadows. He knew beyond any doubt he'd never find a female who would look at him the way Armyn's omega looked at him as he finally released her lips.

Shattered souls and decayed bodies weren't worthy of love. He'd be forever in the dark, always haunted by his own screams and the hiss of burning flesh.

But he wouldn't change his past. He had suffered, but it was worth it. His pain had helped save the others and brought them to their happily ever afters.

No matter how sorry he felt for himself, he wanted his best friend to be happy. Armyn deserved the joy flowing between himself and his new mate. All the men from his unit did.

When the room exploded in a flurry of activity, Quasim realized the festivities had begun. He stalked along the wall, intent on reaching the exit before anyone approached him, but the crowd blocked his path.

Wretched memories and fear immobilized him as the crowd closed in. Trapped in the corner, he locked his eyes on the exit, desperate to escape out into the garden.

Music filled the air. Movement swung his gaze to the stage. A shapely figure emerged from behind the curtain.

Quasim's hardened heart skipped a beat as the omega's skirts began a slow twirl and her arms moved with elegant grace. The delicate antlers atop her head added to her majesty, sweeping through the air as she spun.

No. He didn't just feel a pull toward her.

She stole his darkness and thrust it among the stars, erasing his pain with her elegance and voiding his brokenness with her beauty.

He couldn't turn away. Couldn't refuse the relief she offered him.

He had to have her.

Not for a mate. He couldn't tie such an ethereal creature to the likes of him.

But he needed to soar among the clouds, at least for a little while. She could help him do that.

Her dance ended, leaving her standing in the center of the stage. When she swept her gaze across the crowd, Quasim met her green eyes and knew only one thing.

He needed her to dance for him again.

No matter what it took.

Join V.T. Bonds' newsletter for a STEAMY BONUS SCENE of Cinza and Armyn!

Next in series: Enslaving Ezmira (Sci-Fi Fairytale Fusions Book 4).

***

Buy direct from V.T. Bonds' website and get $1 OFF EVERY E-BOOK. You pay less. I get more.
https://vtbonds.com/product/enslaving-ezmira/

(This discount is approximately what the big retailers take from me per book, so I get more when you buy from my website even though you pay less.)

Author's Note

As our fourth cowrite together, we thought we were prepared for the journey, but these characters floored us. Both Cinza and Armyn surprised and pleased us, pushing their unique voices onto the page. We're overjoyed they found their happily ever afters but can't wait to share with you the book we wrote first—Enslaving Ezmira. Quasim and Ezmira may be the last characters you meet, but they certainly are not the least. As much of an alphahole as Armyn is, Quasim operates on a whole different level. You do not want to miss his story.

If this is your first read from either of us, we hope we've intrigued you enough to seek more from both Leann Ryans and V.T. Bonds. If you're one of our established fans, then hopefully you'll see the unique touch we each brought to the world.

Are you ready for more? Because we are. Always ready to delve into the next steamy, knotty romance novel.

We welcome all devious and depraved souls.

Forever thankful,
Leann Ryans and V.T. Bonds

ENSLAVING EZMIRA

Sci-Fi Fairytale Fusions Book 4

LEANN RYANS AND V.T. BONDS

Enslaving Ezmira (Preview)

Quasim

She crumpled.

He caught her under her arms before she fell out of reach, the sudden movement stealing a hiss of pain from him.

After a ragged breath to regain his senses, he marveled at her delicate features and lithe body. Even as limp as a rag doll, she exuded grace unlike anyone he'd ever met, and she was light as a feather.

She must be an angel who fell through a rainbow.

It took no effort for him to envision a halo resting on the tiny, fuzzy antlers peeking out from her shimmery green hair. No one without divine powers could dance with her passion and suck his pain away.

His memories reared their ugly heads, giving him visions of gleaming metal and red-hot iron, followed by searing agony and evil voices. If it weren't for his brothers' support, he never would have made it out of the enemy's hands alive, and the pain was a daily reminder that he hadn't let the enemy win.

Realizing his fingers dug into delicate flesh, Quasim forced his nightmares aside and lifted the gorgeous omega. He didn't have a plan. He just knew he needed the peace she gave him as she danced.

After settling her face-down over his left shoulder, he ignored the pull of mangled flesh as her slight weight draped down his back. It took a moment of tiny shifts before her dangling shoulder no longer brushed against the stump where his wing once protruded, but eventually he secured her.

He'd only meant to watch her from the shadows, much as he had in the ballroom during her performance, but without the cloying press of the crowd, he'd gotten lost in her scent.

He needed her.

Next in series: *Enslaving Ezmira (Sci-Fi Fairytale Fusions Book 4)*.

***

Buy direct from V.T. Bonds' website and get $1 OFF EVERY E-BOOK. You pay less. I get more.
https://vtbonds.com/product/enslaving-ezmira/

(This discount is approximately what the big retailers take from me per book, so I get more when you buy from my website even though you pay less.)

Unknown Omega

Alpha Elite Series Book 1

V.T. BONDS

Unknown Omega by V.T. Bonds (Preview)

Seeck

A streak of dark brown curls flies past the mouth of the alley.

The blur of her shape rocketing across gives the distinct impression that she's running for her life.

Then her smell hits me. Rich, beautiful, and wrong. A confusing mixture of incompleteness. She should be beta, but she smells of omega.

And blood. I smell the metallic scent and can't stop my body from reacting. My cock grows stiff even as my instincts demand I protect her.

There's the distinct smell of her blood, a puzzle of beauty and pain, and a male's musk clinging to her. His blood mingles with a delicate, specific kind of scent and my body moves of its own accord. The smell of her broken innocence strips all conscious thought from me.

I hurtle up the wall of the decrepit building and launch myself onto the roof. Sprinting, decreasing the space between us, I run over the crumbling structure.

I fling myself over the edge, and the sand buffets my landing. A need fiercer than any rut overwhelms me, so strong that I don't care about my lack of control.

Reaching the front of the alley, I extend my arm and brace for impact.

She runs straight into it, but she's so small that I barely register the hit.

I snatch her out of the air, surrounding her with my arms, clutching her to my chest.

Before she can regain her breath, I drag her deeper into the narrow passage. My hand clamps over her mouth and chin.

Having her so close shreds my hold on reality. Seeing the wild array of hair short circuits my thoughts. Smelling her body and pain within my arms causes a well of need to burst inside me.

I push her against the wall and her cry of pain and fright dampens my need a bit. I meet her eyes and the world shifts.

Everything makes sense. She's mine. My own. My other half. My Omega. My weakness.

Continue reading *Unknown Omega (Alpha Elite Series Book 1)* direct from V.T. Bonds' website for an exclusive discount:

https://vtbonds.com/product/unknownomega/

Monster's Find

Monsters in the Mountains Book 1

Leann Ryans

Monster's Find by Leann Ryans (Preview)

Sasha

"Don't let me interrupt you, little omega. I was enjoying the show." The gruff voice echoed through the darkness, ripping a gasp from me as I scrambled to my belly and backed away from the sound. My entire body throbbed with denied need as I crouched and tried desperately to see the source. A small part of my brain recognized I was in danger, but my body's response was to release more slick to coat my thighs.

Like that would save me.

The next cramp threatened to tear my body in half, pulling my focus back to myself as the muscles in my middle rippled and forced me into a ball of misery at the edge of my pitiful nest. Whoever had spoken wasn't someone I recognized, and I was beyond the point of being able to run.

"Please..."

It was the only word I could force past trembling lips, and even I didn't know what I was asking for. Part of me demanded I send the male away, while another part wanted me to present and beg him for relief. The deepness of the voice and the scent surrounding me left no question the speaker was an alpha, and it didn't matter that he was a stranger.

I *needed*.

"Please what, little one? Are you in distress?"

A whimper was my only response. With the pheromones of the male taking effect in my brain, the cramps became nonstop, one rolling in on the heels of the last, leaving me breathless and crying into the thin grass covering the stone. My core clenched over and over, demanding to be filled with thick alpha cock.

The same scraping sound I'd heard before came closer, stopping at the edge of the little depression I'd claimed for my nest. A low growl left my throat before I could stop it, but it was met with a chuckle from the hulking male I sensed just outside my temporary bed.

"Temper, temper! I'm only offering to give you what you want."

There was a strange accent to the words the male spoke, but they were clear enough to understand. Despite the delicious scent rolling off him and the demands of my body, it was instinct to protect my nest, even as pitiful as it was, until the alpha proved himself.

There still wasn't any light in the cave, but the male's presence was enough for my eyes to lock on to where I assumed he stood. A sense of motion caused me to flinch further away, but there were no more scraping footsteps, and nothing touched me.

He waited.

Another harsh cramp broke my focus again, the desire between my thighs growing more desperate with each breath filled with the male's musk. My hand slipped to my core without conscious thought, two fingers dipping into my entrance to ease the pain but only succeeding in making me more miserable.

It wasn't enough. I needed more.

I couldn't last through days of this. It was torture. I was going to die in misery.

I pushed another finger into my opening, ignoring the alpha's presence as I thrust in and out with desperation. The wet sounds would have embarrassed me at any other time, but they barely registered as my world narrowed to the tension coiled through my belly. Something had to give, and I was scared it would be me, giving in to the male lurking so close.

A soft moan escaped my throat as my knuckles stretched my entrance, but it still wasn't enough. My fingers were too short. Too thin.

"Poor omega. I have what your body craves, if only you'd let me into your nest."

I snarled toward the male, turning my back to where the voice originated. It came from lower than it had before, and I could picture him crouching on the edge of my nest, watching as I tried to ease the ache.

Waiting for the inevitable.

His scent was divine. There was a saltiness to it now that spoke of virility. That called to the animal part of me and told me this was a male in his prime.

A male worth submitting to.

I panted as my fingers worked, wrist starting to ache. Free hand braced against the stone edge of my wallow, I rode my thrusting digits, but it couldn't provide the stretch or the friction my nature demanded. Even adding my little finger to the other three did nothing.

I needed a knot.

Time had no meaning in the desperate daze I'd fallen into. It could have been hours, or days, or mere breaths that passed in my search for relief before I finally collapsed with a sob, my hand stilling. I'd almost forgotten about the male perched at the side of my nest until he spoke again.

"Give in, little one. Let me soothe your pain."

"I will submit to no man."

My hiss was weak, mocking as it echoed back to me even as a chuckle rumbled overtop it.

"Well, *I* am no *man*."

Continue reading *Monster's Find (Monsters in the Mountains Book 1)* by Leann Ryans:

https://books2read.com/monsters-find-1

RESCUED AND RUINED

Warrior Elite Series Book 1

V.T. BONDS

Rescued and Ruined by V.T. Bonds (Preview)

Craize

Something calls me. Blood rains down the walls. Crimson colors the ceiling.

I sink into a rage just as potent as what I felt as I watched my race being caught. A fury as explosive as the anger I felt upon hearing they were experimented on and slaughtered in the most disgusting ways possible.

My shriveled soul expands, seeking the source of whatever beckons me.

The weight of mountains presses down on the ceiling, every step deeper into the facility adding to the oppressive sense of claustrophobia. Not caring whether my teammates follow on my heels or turn to find relief in the sky, I murder any individual in my path. When a large, circular concrete door blocks my path, a roar bursts from my chest, making the fluorescent lights shake within their moors. I crank the lever and rip the offending material from its hinges and toss it away, snarling as the ground beneath me vibrates with its landing.

The hall beyond lacks the stark lighting of those behind me, even the red emergency lights bright compared to the ones below. Ominous dread wafts up from the tunnel, carrying scents of despair and death.

I cross the threshold, my hope dead long ago, my life ruled by hatred and pain. My salvation lies within this darkness. It shrieks in misery, begging me to end its suffering.

Ignoring the doors lining the hall, I continue into the bowels of hell, prepared to desecrate any monsters residing within such an abhorrent place. I follow my screaming instincts, the invisible lead yanking me toward the last door on the left.

It bursts inward in shards of metal and wood, my boot cracking it down the middle. The two ends warp the doorway, the right half tilting and falling as the lock snaps under the weight while the left swings on precarious hinges.

Jumping through the wrecked vestibule long before the last of the fragments hit the once-smooth flooring, my hackles rise as the most feral snarl rips through the air. It isn't until the cloud of debris almost settles that I realize the ache in my throat is from creating the animalistic sound, but my logical mind stands no chance against the need to find whatever lured me here.

Ugly brown orbs appear out of the dust, a human male baring his puny teeth at me in challenge. His dark clothing hides most of his form, but a triangle reveals his jutting cock, the tip spurting acrid liquid.

As he swings his fist despite his eyes popping wide in terror, I grab the sides of his head and slam my forehead down on his.

Gore squishes between us as the pattern of short horns on my forehead embed themselves into his skull, their jagged edges sliding through his bone as though it were butter. I avoid the putrid liquid leaking from his manhood but glory in shedding his lifeblood, jerking my head back and watching as crimson paints his face.

His fist thumps against my side even as his legs begin to crumple. I grab his neck and squeeze, adding another hand and wrenching his trachea.

He thumps to the ground, his neck at an odd angle and his eyes clouding over.

Movement and sounds of struggle break my satisfied stare, and the agony in my chest pulls me further into the room.

A tiny form contorts on a filthy mattress, her white flesh blending into its surroundings despite her vicious lurching.

I step closer, my senses zeroing in on the figure, the pull behind my sternum demanding I reach her. Pert breasts wobble and trim legs create the most luscious form I've ever seen, and even as my conscience screams within my hijacked mind, basal needs demand I take. Claim. Own.

I stalk forward and pin a slim ankle to the mattress.

Bright green irises pierce mine, abject misery shining from a face too delicate for words.

She's the reason I'm here. She called me.

Somehow, she reached into my soul and beckoned me into the pits of hell.

She's *mine*.

Continue reading *Rescued and Ruined (Warrior Elite Series Book 1)* direct from V.T. Bonds' website for an exclusive discount:

https://vtbonds.com/product/rescuedandruined/

TEMPTING A KNIGHT

Hell's Knights MC Book 1

LEANN RYANS

Tempting A Knight by Leann Ryans (Preview)

Brooke

I needed help.

I bit my lower lip to stop it from trembling. Blinking back tears, I dropped my gaze to the stained concrete, trying to come up with something to convince Sebastian to agree. This was the only plan that had a chance of working.

Before I could think of a valid argument, a large hand landed on my shoulder, startling a small yelp from my throat before I could choke it back. Spun around to face the open garage doors, I was thrust forward by the hard grip.

Chuckles followed as Sebastian marched me out of his garage. The size of it proved how well the business had done, and it provided a place for his motorcycle club to hang out during the day. I didn't know much about the Hell's Knights, but they were discussed in whispers just as much as the Purists. The main difference was that Sebastian's club was more inclusive and respected by the average person, while the Purists were hated except by sympathizers.

Sebastian didn't release my shoulder until I cleared the building, and I took two more steps before turning to face him again once he let me go. His ridicule would be better than what I'd face with Arik if I didn't find a way out of his reach.

"Please."

The whisper was pathetic, and shame burned my cheeks as I resorted to begging.

Omegas were desired, shifter or not. They bore whatever they mated with, so there was plenty of interbreeding. I should have had alphas fighting over me, not be forced to beg one to take pity on me and see me through my heat to save me from another.

The problem was finding someone who didn't answer to the Purists, wouldn't claim me, and wouldn't enjoy hurting me.

Movement to the right caught my attention but I ignored it to keep my gaze locked on the man in front of me. Even if they were Knights and a better choice than Arik, the others weren't who I was here for. It was hard enough to place my trust in a man I barely knew, but my brother had trusted Sebastian.

"Just for this cycle. I'll figure out something else before the next. I'm not asking you to claim me or do anything more. It's just a couple days."

Sebastian's eyes narrowed, his features hardening, but he remained silent. The figure who'd approached from the side stepped into my field of vision, another grease-stained alpha, though smaller than Sebastian. His stringy hair was slicked back from a narrow face, his grin sporting missing teeth despite being around my age.

"I'll tend you through your heat, pretty. You say when and where, and my knot is yours."

A shudder rolled down my spine at his leer, the way his eyes focused on my breasts as he adjusted his crotch making my stomach surge. The scent of something wet and dirty rolled off him, gagging me further. I parted my lips to form a denial, but a harsh growl rumbled through the air before the words could emerge from my throat.

Hands clutching my belly as it spasmed, I fought to stay upright under the weight of an alpha's displeasure. As civilized as people tried to pretend they were, we were still animals at our core, and instincts were impossible to ignore.

There were different kinds of growls, but this one was clearly full of rage, and it took a moment before I realized it came from Sebastian but wasn't aimed at me.

Dark eyes locked on the second male, lips pulled back in a snarl as his canines elongated, the noise continued until the other alpha bowed his head and backed away, apology lost under the grating noise assaulting my nerves. Trembling, I stared at the ground and sucked in great gasps of air when it finally faded away, drenched in sweat and on the verge of tears.

I didn't notice Sebastian move closer until his boots appeared on the concrete in front of me. Dragging my gaze up his body until my head tipped back, I was hit once again with how large he was. Human alphas were big, but shifter alphas tended to be even more massive.

Unlike the other male who'd approached, Sebastian's scent wasn't revolting. It wrapped around me, filling my lungs with each inhale and making my eyes want to roll back in my head as I shuddered.

The omega part of me knew this was a strong, dominant male and was ready to roll over and present for him at the first sign of acceptance. The wholly female part enjoyed all that was before me. He was everything an alpha should be. Everything

I desired rolled into one delicious package that I shouldn't want beyond what I needed him for.

"Go home, Brooke, this isn't the place for you. You're better than this. Vincent would be disappointed."

Continue reading *Tempting A Knight (Hell's Knights MC Book 1)* by Leann Ryans:

https://books2read.com/tempting-a-knight

Follow V.T. Bonds

V.T. Bonds is a two-time USA Today Bestselling Author of dark and dirty contemporary, paranormal, and sci-fi romance. As a female veteran and mom of five kids, she enjoys writing filthy, action-packed romances with strong females and possessive alphas.

Go to https://vtbonds.com for a complete list of books by V.T. Bonds.

For new releases, discounts, and Knotty Exclusives, subscribe to V.T. Bonds' newsletter at https://vtbonds.com/newslettersubscriber.

***

Other places to follow V.T. Bonds:

Bookbub Goodreads Facebook

***

Embrace the dark, filthy side of omegaverse.

Brought to you by V.T. Bonds, The Knottiverse is a universe full of nesting, knots, morally grey alphas, and omegas who become the center of their mate's world.

Guaranteed to leave you slick, each story contains an HEA and at least one larger-than-life alpha.

Enter The Knottiverse now at:

https://vtbonds.com/the-knottiverse/

Follow Leann Ryans

I'm a wife and mother of four who's been an avid reader since I could pick up a book. It wasn't unusual for me to read a book a day, ignoring the real world as I was sucked into the pages of a great story.

I grew up on sci-fi and fantasy books before discovering the world of romance. PNR has always been my go-to, and omegaverse is my addiction of choice.

I love writing books featuring heroes who are a bit rough around the edges but aren't overly cruel. My heroines aren't always the take charge type, but neither are all women. They are comfortable in their femininity.

If you're looking for a story that has dark themes without leaving you wanting to punch the hero in the face, mine just might be for you.

***

To see Leann Ryans' full catalog, including books not available on all retailers, check out https://leannryans.com.

Milton Keynes UK
Ingram Content Group UK Ltd.
UKHW021917281024
450365UK00017B/829